Leap of Faith

Wildflower Valley Book 1
Kate Hewitt

Feathers Press

Feathers Press.

Cover design by Rachel Lilly and Charlotte Swartz.

Chapter One

They say there is a spender and a saver in every marriage, but that's just a nicer way of saying one person is sensible, and one person... isn't.

At least that's what I'm thinking when my husband Josh comes bounding into the kitchen one gray February afternoon, a look of excited determination on his face. It's a look I know well, and it usually means I need to brace myself.

"Abby," he says. "I have an idea."

My husband has a lot of ideas. After nineteen years of marriage, I've learned to listen to them with a *mostly* undisturbed equilibrium because often these ideas peter out without too much fanfare or fuss, although occasionally they've sputtered on longer than they should have, which takes another, more stalwart kind of patience.

"Okay," I say as I start slicing some mushrooms for the casserole we're having for dinner, even though two out of my four children don't like mushrooms. *I* like them. I glance into the adjoining family room, to see if any of our four kids is sprawled there, listening with a silent, wide-eyed alertness, because they have the unfortunate tendency of either reacting with melodramatic horror to Josh's idea (moving to the Falkland Islands) or unfettered excitement (buying a school bus and tricking it out like an RV to travel the country) and neither is helpful when it comes to the notions that can occasionally grip Josh like a fever.

"Okay," he says, standing in front of the kitchen counter, one hand upraised like he's about to bestow a blessing. "Hear me out."

"Of course," I murmur, and reach for another mushroom.

"The world," he intones, suddenly turning newscaster-solemn, "is a dark place."

A giggle escapes me before I can help it. I know I need to take all of Josh's ideas seriously because they're important to him, but right now he sounds like the voiceover of a B-list disaster movie.

"Sorry," I say quickly. "It's just... you sounded so serious."

He places both hands flat on the counter, looming over me a little as I reach for an onion. Six mushrooms will try my two mushroom-averse kids enough; they'll push them to the side of their plate, anyway, and I'll end up eating them, which is a lot of mushrooms for one person.

"Abby," Josh says, "I *am* serious. Don't you see it all around us? Politics, social media, epidemic homelessness, the collapse of our cities, the problems with opioid addiction..."

"Okay, hold on." Now I'm the one holding up my hand, but more like I'm warding off a curse. "Now you're just depressing me."

He shakes his head, mournful now. "It's all real, Abs. It's really happening, all around us. Even here, in New Jersey. You know death from synthetic opioids in this state has risen by ninety-seven percent in the last three years?"

"Okay, that's *seriously* depressing." Josh's ideas are usually a little more upbeat than this. "So what does this have to do with your idea?" I ask as I slice into the onion. "Unless you're somehow planning to solve all the world's problems?"

"If only." He smiles wryly before blinking and reeling back. "That onion is strong," he remarks as he wipes his eyes. "How do you do it?"

"Heart of steel," I quip. "I never cry." Which is kind of true. I'm the practical one in our marriage; Josh is the dreamer and emoter. The kids have long had a saying—'if you want the truth, ask Mom. If you want to feel good about yourself, ask Dad.' I'm kind of proud of my side of that equation.

"All right," I tell Josh as I dump the sliced onion into the frying pan, "so hit me with this big idea of yours. I'm ready." I have a feeling this one is going to be a doozy, up there with moving to the Falkland Islands. Josh wanted us all to work on a sheep station five hundred miles off the coast of Antarctica to 'develop the kids' resilience'. It's so remote they would have had to have school by *radio*, and we would have traveled to the one tiny town, Port Stanley, by helicopter. The logistics of such a life eventually defeated even Josh. I told him there were other, less drastic ways to develop our kids' resilience... Although, truth be told, I have yet to figure out what they are.

"Okay." He takes a deep breath. "I want us to try self-sustainable living." He stops, swelling with import as he waits for my response, but I'm not sure what to say because I only sort of know what self-sustainable living really means.

"Okay..." I say slowly as I stir the onions and mushrooms, inhaling their comforting fragrance. "You mean, like us having a vegetable garden?" My thumb is not particularly green, but I've managed to keep our houseplants alive. Mostly. If that's his idea, I think, this is doable. Potentially. I mean, I could theoretically agree to tilling up half of the backyard if he really wanted to.

"Not exactly," Josh replies, with a slightly sheepish smile I know well. "I mean... more like homesteading."

"*Homesteading*?" I repeat incredulously. I am picturing the opening credits of *Little House on the Prairie*, Carrie tumbling down a hill strewn with wildflowers and Ma and Pa Ingalls gazing proudly at their plot of Minnesotan land from the seat of a Conestoga wagon. All tellingly filmed in southern California. "Homesteading," I clarify, "in suburban New Jersey?" We own almost half an acre, which is a decent amount of land for the suburbs, but it's not homesteading territory, surely. And while I just mentally agreed to tilling up part of the backyard, I don't want to turn the whole thing into a cornfield, although I *guess* it could be possible...

"No, not here in New Jersey," Josh says, his tone a mix of insistence and apology. "Somewhere else. I was thinking West Virginia because the land is cheaper, but there are a few options. Tennessee or northern Georgia—"

"You mean *move*?" Shock reverberates through my voice as I still in my slicing. Of course this is not the first time Josh has suggested moving. The Falkland Islands idea lasted a good few weeks, and then there was the school bus/RV idea, as well as a foray into considering living in Poland, of all places, I'm not sure why. Something to do with the cost of living and friendliness to Americans. So, really, I don't know why I'm so surprised Josh is suggesting such a thing now. Maybe because it's been a few years since he last floated a crazy idea like that, and part of me hoped we were past that phase of life.

"Yes, move," Josh replies patiently. "We can't exactly homestead in suburban New Jersey...!" He gives a hearty laugh, like *I'm* the ridiculous one. Meanwhile, I am starting to feel panicked. *Move*? To *homestead...*?

And so I am already shaking my head. "Josh... Bethany is in

eleventh grade." Bethany is our oldest, followed by William at four-teen, Jack at ten, and little Rose at only six. We can't possibly disrupt all of their education.

Josh is already nodding his understanding. "Think how good this will look on her college applications."

I let out a laugh of my own, of disbelief. "Seriously?"

"You know she'll be thinking about it," Josh tells me with a shrug, which of course is true.

Our oldest daughter is semi-obsessed with her college applica-tions. She wants to get into an Ivy League, and so everything she does—from joining extracurricular clubs (Debate and Model UN) to choosing what books she reads (cutting edge contemporary and 'undiscovered' classics) and even what movies she watches (black and white or foreign, only)—is oriented toward that all-important application. Both Josh and I know it's not healthy, but trying to get her to dial it down seems just to make her more frenetic.

Last summer, she wanted us to go to a hurricane-hit region and help rebuild houses for our family vacation, just so she could put it on her application. I did consider it, since it seemed a worthy thing to do, but when I spoke to some relief agencies they kindly suggested that bringing along Rose, who was five years old at the time, was not actually the most helpful thing, surprise, surprise. Also, doing relief work for your own sake rather than the people you're helping kind of defeats the purpose, not that I have been able to get Bethany to appreciate that. Yet.

I've often wondered if it's living in the vicinity of Princeton that's pushed her over the edge. Everything is high-octane competitive here. The competitive sports teams start at age *six*, and to be fair to Bethany, I don't know a single high school student in this area who doesn't base their decisions on how good something will look on their college application. It is inspiring and dispiriting in turns, depending on my mood.

"And what about William?" I press. He's fourteen, on the shyer side and dedicated to his community chess club, and he doesn't take to change well. He was the one who reacted to the Falkland Islands proposal with undisguised and acute horror. Actually, they pretty much all did, except for Rose, who was only two at the time and understandably didn't know where the Falklands Islands *were*. I hadn't even been sure where they were until I looked at a map, and then I was as horrified as William.

"William can play chess in West Virginia or wherever we decide to move," Josh says as he spreads his hands wide. "There will be clubs there. Maybe even better ones. You know how cutthroat it is here, and how that can get him down."

Last year, William was beaten by a seven-year-old with her own personal coach. That's the kind of place   we live in   .

"Why West Virginia, exactly?" I don't know why I'm humoring him so much; I already know I'm going to shut this one down ASAP. We are not moving our entire lives to West Virginia or *wherever* so we can grow our own vegetables and attempt to live off grid. We're just not.

"Like I said, it doesn't have to be West Virginia," Josh says quickly, his tone turning cajoling. He leans back over the counter as I unscrew the lid on a jar of spaghetti sauce. "I was originally thinking Alaska, but—"

"Not Alaska."

"Done."

I shake my head, weary now. Sometimes I'm in the mood to

humor Josh, to go along with him a little bit. It's a game we play, and it can be nice to dream. I let him spin the fantasy and I enter into it for a few minutes or hours or sometimes even days or weeks. The school bus/camper van scenario was particularly appealing; I've always wanted to travel across North America. I just didn't want to give up my entire life to do it.

This, however, is not one of those times. Bethany is taking the SAT this Saturday, and William is in a chess tournament in Morristown. Next week Jack has his final assessment for ADHD at one of the best hospitals in the country, which is practically on our doorstep, after months of appointments. And Rose, at only six, has a best friend named Chloe that I know she would be devastated to leave behind.

Ten years ago, when Josh first started floating some of his crazy ideas, they seemed a little more possible because our kids were little and we could move around more easily, at least in *theory*. The fact that we never did isn't the point; the point is that *now*, when we're embedded into this community in a dozen different ways, when we've put down roots that have become deep and long-lasting, it's neither easy nor appealing.

In fact, it's ridiculous, not that I'll be as cruel to say that outright to my idealistic, dream-driven husband whom I love very much.

"I'm not so sure, Josh." I dump the sauce into the pot and stir halfheartedly. I can *feel* him getting all his arguments ready, like a row of tin soldiers I'll have to knock down one by one, and I really don't have the time or energy for that now. "I mean," I continue quickly, before he can speak, "it sounds kind of fun, and I know we've talked about that kind of life while we're watching *Alone*..." All eleven seasons; that much survivalist television can really mess with your head. "But," I finish, firming my voice to let him know I mean it, "It's just not feasible now. Not with everything we have going on here. The kids are all happy in their schools, we're over halfway through paying off our mortgage, we've both got jobs..." I trail off, but not long enough for him to jump in with his arguments—that we're not thrilled with the public school system in our township; my job is remote, and Josh's is hybrid; having paid off more than half the mortgage would mean we'd get a lot of money if we sold, and the property market is hot right now.

I know Josh so well that I could make these arguments myself, and they would be compelling. Well, *somewhat*. But   I already know I don't want to let myself be swayed, not even a little bit, and even though I feel guilty for being so uncharacteristically blunt, I decide to   nip this in the bud and burst my husband's happy balloon, just to confuse my metaphors.

"We're not moving anywhere," I tell him, a pronouncement. "And that's that."

Chapter Two

Josh and I met in college. I was a bit like Bethany—head down, studying hard, trying to hide my ever-present anxiety with more admirable-seeming ambitious determination. Josh was the dreamer, idealistic and laidback, always ready to go on an adventure, no matter how seemingly small—or silly. Our romance started when we were taking the same class sophomore year—a deadly dull economics class that Josh was taking to fulfill a requirement, while I was in the hopes of one day getting a good job.

It was a beautiful April afternoon in Vermont—we went to a small liberal arts college with the most idyllic, New Englandy campus you could imagine—and as we naturally fell into step to enter the building, Josh turned to me and said, "Hey, you want to cut class and get an ice cream?"

At this point, we'd never spoken to each other. I was *aware* of Josh, as a guy in my class who was pretty good-looking, with his floppy brown hair and glinting hazel eyes, a smile that seemed to tug at his mouth without him even realizing. I also knew he had some snappy comebacks for our professor that were funny without being rude, mainly because Josh said them in such a whimsical tone. There has always been something very *likeable* about my husband, which is probably why I did something I had never done before and would never consider doing again for that entire year and said yes.

At the door to the building, we turned and strode away like we had somewhere to go. And in fact, we did—the old-fashioned ice cream parlor in town, where Josh bought me a double scoop of raspberry cheesecake ice cream (I had decided at that point that if I was going to cut class I might as well make the most of it and went for a flavor I'd never tried before) and then we wandered down to the old wooden bridge that spanned the river that ran through town, and sat on it with our legs dangling down and ate our ice cream cones with the spring sunshine bathing us in golden light.

It's still one of my happiest memories.

I don't remember all that much about our conversation, truth be told, only that Josh asked me questions and listened intently to my answers. I remember how intent and interested he sounded when he asked me what I wanted to do with my life, how admirable his own ambitions seemed, how easy his enjoyment of the world around us, from the sun shining above to the ice cream cones we were eating—me with careful little bites, Josh with obvious gusto.

"I want to do everything," he told me, as if such a thing were possible. "Travel, explore, work... I want to build my own house and sail around the world and learn to fly a plane." He laughed while I stared at him uncertainly, unsure if he was being serious. "Why not?" he continued, the words flung to the blue sky above us. "I mean, seriously, why not?" He lowered his head to look at me then as if waiting for an answer, but I was too tongue-tied to give him one.

"I... I guess there's no reason," I finally said hesitantly, feeling like I was disappointing him already. "Except, you know, maybe time and opportunity and money."

"Exactly," he replied, as if these were insignificant obstacles, and maybe they were. It was an entirely new way of thinking to me, and one that was equally alarming and exciting. To Josh, life seemed like a cornucopia of opportunities to marvel at and plunge into. I wanted to feel that way too, if only a little bit. Twenty-two years on, I've learned that it is wonderful living with someone like that, but it can also be occasionally exhausting.

By the end of that conversation, I was feeling sun-warmed and happy, but also wistful that my future was, by my own making, so very *planned*, as well as anxious that I'd skipped the class, worrying I wouldn't find someone who would be willing to share their notes.

As we strolled back towards campus, Josh reached for my hand and twined his fingers through mine like it was the most natural thing in the world, sending sparks zinging through my whole body. "Let's do this again," he said, and I shot back automatically,

"I am *not* skipping class again."

He laughed, a pure sound of joyful amusement. "We'll see."

I didn't skip class again, but we did go for a hike through the Green Mountains, complete with picnic, that weekend. In addition to being a dreamer, Josh is a wonderful romantic. Our first kiss was on a picnic blanket, the mountains our stunning backdrop, the moment the sweetest I could have wished for.

We were engaged by the end of our junior year; married the summer we graduated. And in the twenty-two years since we've known each other, Josh has continued to take me on adventures—some bigger than others. Whether it's trying a new flavor of ice cream (bacon flavor is a definite no) or going rollerblading (I nearly killed myself, but I did actually end up enjoying it), he has always gently, and sometimes less gently, pushed me to explore new horizons.

And I like to think I have, in return, grounded him with my

practical pragmatism and helpful reminders that bills need to be paid and living in the same place for seventeen years is actually a *good* thing.

Which is why I decide I'm not budging on this *Homesteading Thing*.

After my shutdown of the conversation as I was making dinner, I was hoping Josh might drop the idea completely. Sometimes these whims come and go in the course of an evening—starting a landscaping business as a 'side hustle' and agreeing to not buy anything new except for food for an entire year being among the ideas that thankfully had a very short shelf life.

This one, however, seemed to have a little more staying power.

That night, as we are getting ready for bed, my mind on my to-do list tomorrow which included fitting in a grocery shop, walking the dog, and six hours of paid work all within the seven hours of the school day, Josh mentions it again.

"I know you think it's crazy," he tells me, holding up a hand to forestall my immediate response, "but can we at least talk about my idea seriously? Put aside some time and really consider what I'm saying?"

"Is this about the homesteading thing again?" I ask through a mouthful of toothpaste, which isn't fair of me, because I know it is, but I am being dismissive on purpose. I just really do not want to consider this one seriously. It's right up there with the Falkland Islands, as far as I'm concerned. West Virginia? It might as well be hovering near the coast of Antarctica. Our lives are *here*.

"Yes, it's about the *homesteading thing* again," Josh replies, his voice very slightly edged with irritation. He needs me to take these things seriously. I know he does, and so I feel guilty, which makes me say grudgingly,

"All right, we can talk about it seriously. When were you thinking?"

"How about dinner, just you and me, Friday night? A date."

A date where I'll spend the whole evening thinking of ways to dissuade my husband from pursuing this ridiculous plan. *Sounds fun*, I think, but I manage a smile and nod. Josh deserves a little more openness from me, even if I am finding it hard to give it. I need to try.

"Okay," I say, managing a smile. "Friday it is."

I put it out of my mind for the next three days, because life is that busy. Josh works as an accountant—something I admittedly pushed him toward for the stability after a couple of years of goofing around, including a backpacking trip through Europe for an extended honeymoon—and I'm a bookkeeper, which might be two of the most boring-sounding jobs in the world, but they pay the bills, and I like working with numbers. I especially like seeing figures add up.

It gives me a sense of stability and even sanity in a world that can, as Josh intoned when he first brought up the homesteading thing, seem dark and chaotic. I can admit he's right in *that*, at least, even if the rest is crazy.

It's not until Friday afternoon when William asks what we're doing that evening and if we can have takeout pizza that I remember the whole date.

"Dad and I are actually going out tonight," I tell him in something of an apology, because Josh and I go out so little that when we do, the kids are both taken aback and a little alarmed, like we're trekking across Siberia rather than heading down to our local watering hole. "But yes," I add, "you can have pizza."

"Where are you going?" William asks as he slides onto a stool at the kitchen island. His dark hair, the same color as mine, is sliding into his face, and he blinks at me from behind his glasses. William is a self-proclaimed geek; in elementary school, he was proud of all his seemingly geeky accomplishments—chess club, an interest in bugs, high mathematical ability, lack of athletic prowess or interest in sports. Then he entered middle school and suddenly started seeing everything he loved as a liability. For about six months of sixth grade, he floundered between feeling like he needed to try to be cool and wanting to embrace his own seemingly eccentric interests.

In spring of that year, it all came to a head when a class bully broke the microscope he'd brought to school to show his science teacher; parents were called in, terms negotiated. The bully had to apologize (big deal), and William was told not to bring anything valuable into school ever again, not exactly the most helpful takeaway from that encounter, as far as I was concerned.

The episode acted as a catalyst of sorts, catapulting William into embracing his full, geeky self. No more trying to be cool, he doubled down on everything he loved—joining the chess club and starting an entomology group, which grew to an impressive eight members. I'm   proud of him for persevering against bullies as well as sticking to his guns about who he is and what's important to him, but I still worry.

He's fourteen now, halfway through ninth grade, and while high school wasn't quite the bumpy transition middle school was, it hasn't exactly been smooth sailing. William decided against starting an entomology club in the high school ('No one's interested in bugs anymore, Mom') and he does chess at the community library because his high school doesn't have a chess club. He hasn't found his tribe yet—his two best friends from middle school went private for high school, a common occurrence in this area—and although he's never complained, I worry he feels a little adrift in a sea of jocks and cheerleaders, although, to be fair, his high school has plenty of academically-driven nerdy types. William just doesn't seem to have become friends with any of those kids. Yet.

Which is why I suggest, in the sort of jolly tone I know teenagers can see right through, "you could invite someone over if you wanted, to watch a movie or something?"

William, understandably, looks at me like I've suggested he take off all his clothes and parade down Nassau Street, the main thoroughfare of Princeton. He has never asked someone over to watch a movie 'or something', and so my suggestion is not even worthy of a reply.

"Can I get my own triple pepperoni pizza?" he asks instead, and I hold in the sigh that is threatening to escape in a long, lonely gust. When will I learn that my children are who they are, and I cannot change them with kindly meant (i.e. semi-manipulative) suggestions?

"Sure, sweetie," I say.

I order the pizza and then head upstairs to change for Josh's and my *date*. It doesn't feel date-like, and so I'm unsure what to wear. Usually when we go on dates (the last one was at least six months ago), I try to wear something a *little* dressy—my one cashmere sweater, perhaps, or a pair of skinnier-than-usual jeans. Something to show I'm making an effort, up to a point, because The Tiger's Tale does not warrant an actual *outfit*. Most people in there are slouched at the bar wearing baseball caps and old jeans.

I pull out the cashmere sweater and my bootleg jeans. I stopped wearing skinny jeans when I turned forty, but in any case, Bethany informed me that nobody wears them anymore, so I am unexpectedly on trend.

I battle a feeling of something close to dread as I brush my teeth and slap on some concealer and mascara, the *only* makeup to wear after forty, according to somebody on Instagram. I tell myself I don't need to be so negative about tonight; I can hear my husband out, even run with it a little. All of Josh's ideas peter out eventually. I can be patient. I don't need to shut him down *right* away... even if twenty-four hours have merely cemented my certainty that we are *not* upending our lives, moving house, and reenacting some twenty-first century version of *Little House on the Prairie*. No way.

"Abby?" Josh's voice floats up the stairs as I stand back from my reflection and give it a sort of grimacing, it'll-do nod. For forty-two, I don't look too bad. Not bad at all, I tell myself, and then I stiffen my spine to head downstairs and face my husband.

Chapter Three

The Tiger's Tale is three miles from our house and has been, mainly by default, our local. It's always crowded, boisterous and affable, and the food is decent—think Chili's or TGI Friday's, but a bit more personalized. I especially recommend their Peruvian jumbo shrimp.

Josh and I don't talk about homesteading during the drive. We keep the conversation light, conducting the usual evening check-in about our children.

"Bethany aced her history test," Josh remarks with pride.

No surprise there. "Jack's been invited to Grayson's house next week," I inform him, and he frowns.

"Grayson... Is that..."

"He's okay," I say quickly. Some of the boys in Jack's class are a little... boisterous. As is he, so being around similar boys doesn't help, although it's a bit of a pot and kettle situation.

"Rose have a good day at school?" Josh asks.

"I think so."

Rose is our surprise baby, five years younger than Jack. We'd thought our family was complete, but obviously it wasn't. Rose usually falls in with everyone else, mainly because she doesn't really have a choice, although up until the age of two she was a colicky, difficult baby who cried all the time, and so, with the pregnancy which was also challenging, I basically feel like I missed three years of my life.

Everyone was telling me how the golden years of parenting are when your children are all in elementary school—old enough to *do* things, and young enough to still want to do them with you. Sadly, my memory of those years is walking up and down our nursery (it used to be Josh's study), practically comatose with tiredness. Josh would take the older three to do the fun things—movies and bowling and climbing courses—while I stayed home and paced with Rose.

He would gallantly offer to be the one who stayed home, but we both knew how well that would have worked out. Rose wanted her mama, and while I wasn't always thrilled to be stuck at home, Josh has always been the one who loved all the older-kid stuff—wrestling and baseball in the backyard and movies with a big bucket of buttered popcorn to share. He entered into the spirit of the thing far more than I ever could, and the kids have always loved that.

But in any case, those challenging years are now thankfully behind us, which is why we can enjoy the fruits of our labor, those years of hard parenting graft. That, I have decided, is going to be my argument tonight. Why make things harder for ourselves if we don't have to?

We're led to a table in the back, and the waitress leaves us with menus and a promise to be right back, although since the place is absolutely hopping I have a feeling she'll be a while.

"So I know you don't think I'm serious about this," Josh announces without preamble as he peruses the menu, "but I am."

"Okay," I reply, because what else can I say? "I respect that." Josh raises his eyebrows, and I grimace a little. "I mean, I'm *trying* to, but this does seem a little... out there, Josh, even for you." I smile in an attempt to take any sting from my words. We both must know I'm just making an obvious observation.

"I know it is, which is why I wanted to have this chance to talk about it properly," he says, putting down his menu to lean over the table. "Explain everything, how it could work."

How it could work? "You've really thought about this, then," I remark slowly. Usually Josh's ideas remain in the realm of the semi-fantastic, backed up only by a few haphazard internet searches and maybe a podcast, along with a lot of hazy dreaming and vague grand plans.

"I have," he confirms.

The waitress, true to her word, returns, and Josh orders a beer, and I ask for a glass of their house white.

"Small, medium or large?" she asks me, and I try to smile as I reply, "Large." I have a feeling I'm going to need it.

"Okay," I tell Josh once she's left, trying not to visibly brace myself, although I certainly feel the need. "Hit me with your ideas."

He lets out a slightly shaky laugh, and with a ripple of shock, I realize he's nervous. Josh *never* gets nervous. He announces his ideas with the vocal equivalent of a trumpet fanfare, painting glorious pictures of the life we didn't know we always wanted. But if he's nervous now... he really must be serious.

Oh, dear. I think I need that wine.

"I'm not really sure where to begin," he admits. He's picked up a beer mat from the table and is now rotating it around in his hands, his head slightly ducked, his caramel-brown hair sliding into his eyes, the same way it does with William's. For a second I am reminded of the twenty-year-old boy-man I fell in love with, because yes, I did fall in love with him, right on that first walk, when we ate ice cream and talked about our futures. At least, I started to, and maybe I need the reminder of that now, when every hackle I have is raised, and I am ready to shoot down whatever Josh is going to say, practically before he says it.

No wonder he's nervous. We know each other too well for him not to realize that's how I'm feeling.

"When did you start thinking about this?" I ask. I realize I am genuinely curious. How long has this madcap plan been brewing?

"A couple of weeks ago," Josh replies, and I nod.

A couple of *weeks*? Okay, we're in familiar territory here. Surely this will blow over, just as every idea has before. The waitress returns with our drinks, and I take a large, celebratory sip, because I feel so relieved.

"It started with a podcast," Josh tells me.   "About sustainable living—growing your own food, sourcing your own water and electricity. Basically, having a smallholding that provides for all your needs. Do you know you can live off just five acres?"

"I didn't know that," I tell him and take another sip of my wine.

"It resonated with me on a whole lot of levels," Josh continues. "Environmentally, yes, but also socially. I don't like the world our kids are growing up in, Abs. I'm not sure I want them—or us—to be a part of it anymore."

I pause, because this sounds a little more serious, as well as alarming. "So we retreat from all of society?" I ask, making sure to keep my voice reasonable, even gentle. "Circling the wagons never seems like a healthy solution, Josh. I think you'd say that, too."

"I'm not talking about circling the wagons. I don't want to become some kind of gun-toting prepper or start a cult." He gives me his familiar, whimsical smile that *still* has the power to make my stomach curl, even now, when I am doing my best to argue with him. "I just want to live differently. I want our *kids* to live differently." He leans forward, earnest again. "Look at Bethany. She's so obsessed with college applications, proving herself over and over again and never seeming to succeed, at least in her own mind—have you seen her eczema lately? It's all over her arms and legs. She's stressed, Abby, and she's only sixteen." Josh's expression firms. "I want to guide her off the hamster wheel—"

"I thought you said homesteading would *help* her college applications—" I protest.

"Well, that's what we'd tell her." He grins. "And I do think it would, but I'm hoping she chooses another, healthier path in life."

"There's nothing wrong with aiming high," I argue. What kind of path is Josh envisioning? Pioneer woman? "Bethany has ambition," I state. "That's a good thing."

Josh is quiet for a moment as he continues to rotate the beer mat between his fingers. He hasn't taken a single sip of his beer, and I'm halfway through my glass of wine. My large glass of wine. "I'm not sure it is a good thing," he says quietly. "Once I might have agreed with you. But now... I think there's more to life, and she's missing it. We all are."

I am silent, absorbing this. The sentiment is one Josh has shared before; in fact, all his crazy plans have their genesis in the sense that I think almost everyone has, at one time or another, that there must be more to life than what they're currently experiencing. Generally, I find you can ride out that feeling fairly quickly, simply by focusing on what is good in your life, or at least what keeps you busy. But the sense that there must be something more has dogged Josh for most of our marriage, in one lighthearted way or another.

This time *does* feel different... even if he's only been thinking about it for a couple of weeks.

"So you don't want Bethany to go to a good college?" I ask, knowing even as I say it that it's an unreasonable and even childish question, but it's what I fixate on anyway.

"I don't want her to go to a good college if it breaks her as a person," Josh responded levelly. "She's not happy, Abby."

I am silent, because while I know he is right, and that our oldest child has been getting increasingly frantic over the last few months as she gears up for her final year of high school... isn't that just part of life? Applying to college is an intense time. It doesn't mean you up-end an entire family. "And you think homesteading in West Virginia will fix that?" I ask, and this time I don't try to sound reasonable or gentle. I let him hear the skepticism in my voice, because *come on*. "That's not the obvious solution, at least to me."

"Bethany's situation is just a symptom of a greater problem," Josh replies, and I take a sip of wine to keep from rolling my eyes.

I already know what the greater problem has to be—social media, a fast-paced world, politics out of control, and so on. Other people live with these challenges. We can too... without moving anywhere.

"I know you don't want to see it," Josh tells me, and now there is an edge to his voice I am definitely not used to hearing, "but it's there, Abby, and it's consuming us. We go through our days in a frantic blur, falling into bed to snatch a few hours' sleep before we do it all over again. Most of the time we're all miserable and tense, even little Rose, even if we do our best to mask it. *Everything* feels like a hassle, even the things we're meant to enjoy." He stops, as if waiting for me to acknowledge that what he's just said is true, which I don't, even though I know it is. Because that's just *life*. And we can change our attitudes without changing our circumstances, can't we?

"And I for one," Josh resumes, "don't want to keep living this way, treading the same ground, over and over again, and never feeling like I'm getting anywhere. We're both over forty now, we're looking down the barrel, as it were. If we want to do something big, then now's the time."

"But I don't want to do something big," I tell him, trying once more to sound reasonable. "Josh..." I try for a smile. "This is starting to sound like a midlife crisis." I try to make it sound *sort of* like a joke, even though I'm kind of serious.

"This is not a midlife crisis," Josh informs me quietly. "It might sound like one, but I have thought about this. I've researched it. Yes, there's a lot more work to do, and I'm not advising we leap before we look—"

"Really?" I burst out, and he frowns, a look of hurt coming into his hazel eyes.

"Can you take what I'm saying seriously, just for tonight at least?" he asks quietly. "Don't treat this conversation as a way to convince me I'm crazy, Abby, please." I have to look down, ashamed, because that's exactly what I've been doing. I thought I was being subtler about it, but clearly I wasn't. "Just listen and genuinely think about what I'm saying," Josh continues. "Before you try to figure out how you can prove to me this is unnecessary and won't work."

"Okay," I relent on something of a sigh. "I'll try. I admit, I do have a knee-jerk reaction to shut this whole thing down, but... I will try."

"Thank you," Josh says, and he sounds like he means it. I hope I meant what I said, too.

Just then, the waitress comes back for our orders. Josh goes for his usual burger, and I ask for the Peruvian jumbo shrimp—and another glass of wine. Then I turn to my husband with a determined and hopefully encouraging smile and say,

"Okay. Now you can *really* hit me with what you're thinking."

And I brace myself again to listen.

Chapter Four

I am sitting on a hard plastic chair in the waiting room of a labyrinthine warren of medical offices in Princeton Junction, with Jack glued to my phone, playing Bloons TD5, a game that has been around so long even I recognize the luridly colored screen. We've been waiting for his assessment appointment for forty-five minutes; I broke after twenty and gave him my phone. A middle-aged man gave me a look of disapproving scorn when I did; I bet he doesn't have children. In any case, he should understand. Everyone in the waiting room is here to be assessed for ADHD. This has to be one of the few waiting rooms where calmly sitting still is not the norm.

Josh resisted the whole notion of searching for a diagnosis for Jack. "He's a ten-year-old, active little boy," he said with a shrug. "Let him grow out of it."

Well, maybe that would have worked ten, twenty, fifty years ago. But today? Today diagnoses are *needed*, even if it sometimes can seem like they're given out like lollipops, because you can't actually get any help without one. If Jack gets diagnosed with ADHD, he will be able to access behavioral therapy, academic accommodations, and classroom interventions. His teachers will, hopefully, be more understanding of the things that have been on his report card since he was in kindergarten—*Jack has trouble focusing, Jack doesn't use an indoor voice, Jack can be aggressive with friends, Jack can't sit still.* And he won't feel like he's out of sync with everyone else... not, admittedly, that he notices all that much when he is, but I certainly do.

I need this diagnosis as much as my son does, to get him on the right track to a successful future, but as Jack lets out a yowl of frustration when he loses the game, and I have to catch the phone in his hand before he hurls it to the floor, I wonder if it's worth it. Waiting in a room with nothing but hard plastic chairs—not even an old magazine to flip through—is a form of torture for both of us, and I'm not convinced we'll even get a diagnosis today. We've had so many appointments over the last year, each one shunting us down the line, to yet another assessment. This one, with a pediatric psychologist, is meant to be the last one. We had to wait four months for this appointment, so I tell myself another hour won't kill me, but it's definitely testing my patience.

While Jack has been playing on my phone, my thoughts have been on a replay of my conversation with Josh last Friday. Four days on, he still feels strongly about the whole *Homesteading Thing*, as I've come to call it in my mind.

As for how I feel about it... I don't actually know. I still don't want to do something so over the top, of course, and I definitely don't want to move, but...

I keep *thinking* about it. Which is weird, although I tell myself it's just because I'm worried Josh isn't going to let it go all that easily, and I'm not thrilled at the prospect of spending the next six months or so watching YouTube videos on how to keep chickens or build your own self-composting toilet—Josh already forwarded me links to those two, as well as to a podcast on 'Homesteading for Beginners'. The first episode was 'How Homesteading Changed My Life'. I haven't listened to it yet, because I don't want to know how, or even if, it could.

I don't *want* to change my life; I don't want to feel like my life needs changing. The trouble is, after my conversation with Josh on Friday night, I have a terrible, sneaking feeling that if I listen to it, I might actually change my mind. Maybe just a little bit, but it's enough so that I decide not to click on any of the links, even though I told Josh I would.

The doubts started creeping in when, after we ordered our meals, Josh launched into his ideas—not about homesteading itself, how we'd raise chickens and cows and plant corn or *whatever*, but about why he thought we should think about it. He talked about how William was unhappy and hadn't made any friends in high school, something I was uncomfortably aware of but had told myself he just needed time. He said Jack needed more activity to burn off all his energy—not stimulants or behavioral therapy to function in 'the narrow band of educational expectation'. He said Rose needed to learn resilience as well as independence; we'd all got in the habit of doing things for her rather than letting her learn herself. And Bethany, as we discussed before, needed to seriously chill out and refocus her energies on something that was better for her mental wellbeing.

"Okay, okay," I burst out when he paused to take a breath in the middle of this depressing litany. "Those are areas we need to work on, as parents and as a family. But Josh..." How many times did I need to say it? "That doesn't mean we have to move, or *homestead*, for heaven's sake. These are common problems that face every twenty-first century family. We can *deal* with them in a non-drastic way."

He nodded then, like he expected me to say exactly that, and he had his comeback prepared, which he did. "Yes, we'll deal with them," he agreed. "We'll talk to Bethany about being mindful, we'll encourage William to invite someone over, or we'll try to maneuver him into some social situation he will openly dread but that we'll pray flips some kind of switch inside him. We'll sign Jack up for another sport and limit screentime—the sport will just be yet another hassle and carpool to arrange and the screen limiting will probably last for a week, if we're lucky. And for about the same amount of time, we'll make Rose clear her dishes and fold her laundry and then it will all fall apart again, because I'll have a work deadline, or you'll get the flu, or Bethany will freak out about a homework assignment, *something* will happen, and chaos will ensue as it goes back to what we have come to accept as normal." He leaned forward, his gaze intent, maybe even a little angry.

"That's how it *always* is, Abby," he continued. "That's how it has always been. We're all stuck on a hamster wheel, and I want off. I know, I know." He held up a hand to forestall any protests that I might make, although for once I was speechless because he sounds so intense and some part of me was actually resonating with what he was saying, which was seriously alarming.

"We inhabit a system with all of its societal expectations where we *have* to act this way," Josh states, "because everyone else is, and if you're the only one doing it differently it doesn't work. That's why I want to get out of the whole ecosystem. I want to inhabit a different system—one where we're not slaves to the school schedule or work deadlines or screentime or sports. One where we can be together as a family—living, learning, *being*." He leaned forward again, his palms flat on the table. "Don't you want that, too? Forget the homesteading part for a moment—don't you want that kind of life? One where each day isn't something to be endured, but enjoyed? Where we can stop and actually savor things—a meal, a sunset, a moment of laughter—"

"If you think there won't be a schedule involved with farming," I told him, trying to sound wry, "I think you're heading for a big wakeup call. From everything I know, and admittedly it's not that much, farming is seriously hard work."

"It would be a different schedule, though," Josh argued. "One that's in rhythm with nature."

All right, I did roll my eyes then, but at the same time I got what he was saying. Sort of. But farming was relentless work, and there was no money in it. It wasn't like he was suggesting we move to the Caribbean and open a surf shop, not that I wanted to do that. No matter how appealing he might have made it sound, everything in me still resisted. It was just too much—too weird, too random, too different, too hard.

"So in addition to working the land," I asked him, "are you intending that we homeschool?"

Because that's what it had sounded like, with the whole living-and-learning schtick.

Josh shrugged in reply. "That's certainly something I'd want to consider," he said.

Good grief. Here was an added layer of unwelcome surprise. Homeschooling *and* homesteading? *How?* We both had jobs, although mine was part-time, but I'd never seen myself as a homeschooling type. I might have gotten a little teary when Bethany traipsed off onto the big yellow bus to kindergarten, but trust me, I was over it by lunchtime.

And yet...

I couldn't believe there was even an *and yet*. I should have been telling Josh that this was his craziest idea ever, that I would have rather moved to the Falkland Islands or traveled the country on a tricked-out school bus, instead of actually listening to him like I would take this seriously for so much as a second.

And yet. And yet I was, just the teeniest, tiniest bit doing just that. Josh has always had the knack of tapping into that admittedly small part of me that longs to be different. From the moment we met, he's done it, sometimes unthinkingly, sometimes with deliberate and effective intent. He's certainly pushed me in ways I've appreciated, often only in retrospect, but still. There's a difference between doing a half-marathon (I have never been a runner) and *moving to West Virginia to work the land*...! A huge difference.

Why was I entertaining the notion in even the slightest way?

"Jack Bryant?"

The nurse is unsmiling as she stands in the doorway to the consulting rooms, but I beam at her anyway. Finally! I am relieved to be out of this waiting room, and also out of my spiraling thoughts. I want to *do* something productive, and this is it.

"Come on, Jackie." I ruffle his hair and slide the phone from his sweaty grip in a one-two punch I am well-versed in before we stride toward the hallway. Today we're going to get some answers, and they will put paid to all the questions that Josh has raised in my mind like a flock of crows, their beating wings drowning out my usual voice of rationality. At least I *hope* they will do that.

They don't. At least, they don't deal with the questions the way I wanted them to. The pediatric psychologist asks Jack a ton of questions and goes over all the material that's already been amassed—reports from his teachers, his pediatrician, another specialist we saw nearly a year ago now. The psychologist, bearded and thoughtful, steeples his fingers together and speaks in a slow, gentle voice. Part of me is gritting my teeth, wanting him to hurry up and just get to the point. Maybe *I* have ADHD.

Apparently, Jack *might* have it, although the psychologist says he "resists labels", which seems strange, because I thought psychologists were in the business of assigning them. In any case, by the end of the appointment, we have a prescription for low-dose Adderall, a referral for a therapist, several brochures on coping strategies, a book recommendation, and the link to a monthly support group for parents, on Zoom. I feel exhausted by it all, and also strangely dissatisfied. This has helped, sort of, but it hasn't actually *changed* anything. It hasn't changed Jack, which wasn't what I wanted, not exactly, but... I still feel like something's missing, which is how I've felt since Friday night.

It's very annoying.

We drive home through school-day traffic, a snake of cars on Route 1 under a leaden February sky, with every single car refusing to let me in from the merging lane, because this is New Jersey, the land of rude and aggressive drivers. I drum my fingers against the steering wheel as I mutter unintelligibly under my breath.

I'm going to be late picking up Bethany from band practice, which will make me late getting home to William and therefore late taking him to chess club. He hates having to walk into a crowded room when he's late, and so he'll probably refuse to go, and Josh won't be home to cajole him out of it, because he has a work meeting in New York, something that he has to go to once a month. It just so happened that Jack's appointment landed on the same day. What are the chances? Somehow the chances of this kind of scheduling conflict often seem remarkably high.

Then there's Rose, who got home the same time as William; our neighbor met her off the bus but since it's just been William and Rose at home, she'll have been on the iPad for a good two hours, because William is not the most attentive babysitter. He'll also probably have forgotten to let out Max, our Springer spaniel rescue, which means Max *might* have peed in the kitchen. And if I'm really lucky, someone will have stepped in it and not cleaned it up afterward. At the thought, a growl of frustration escapes me.

Jack looks at me askance. "Are you okay, Mom?"

No, I am not okay. The words come unbidden, automatic, and they make me furious. I was perfectly fine until Josh started talking to me about wanting something different. Suddenly my life feels small and tense and *difficult*, and I really don't want it to.

I want to go back to the way I was, but I'm not sure I can, and that's what infuriates—and scares—me most of all.

Chapter Five

During the next hour, everything unfolds exactly the way I feared it would. Bethany is annoyed I was fifteen minutes late picking her up because she has *so* much homework, and William is both morose and resigned to not going to chess club because he cannot possibly walk into the library twenty minutes into the session.

"Everyone will be in the middle of a game, Mom," he explains, his voice high and thin with anxiety. "I'll have nobody to play with and so I'll just have to *wait*."

"Then you can wait," I reply as patiently as I can, but William just shakes his head, resolute.

"No, I couldn't. *Nobody* does that."

"Nobody does what?" Rose asks, looking up from the iPad.

I decide to leave the argument for now as I go to the fridge to see if we have anything I can make for dinner—and step in the puddle of pee I'd missed before. Bethany slams her textbooks onto the kitchen table, still annoyed that I was late because she has *a really important essay due, like, tomorrow.*

The ground beef I was hoping to turn into a casserole is two days past its expiration date and when I sniff it, it definitely smells a little funny, plus it looks kind of gray. I throw it into the trash just as

Rose lets out a yowl of rage as Jack rips the iPad from her hands. William lets out his own groan of malcontent while Bethany shrieks that everyone needs to be quiet, because she has *work* to do.

Of course, I know that none of these things should convince me that we need to sell our house and move to West Virginia. It's just a normal, slightly chaotic evening in the life of a normal, slightly chaotic family. Nothing to see here, not really, and yet...

There it is again, that *and yet* that is dogging all my days, because after I've read Rose three stories—she asks for the same ones every night, which is a tiny bit worrying—and have tucked her into bed, and then made sure Jack is getting into the shower and both William and Bethany are doing their homework, I retreat to the window seat in the dining room with my laptop. It is a space that is private and has a nice view of the backyard, the slightly depressing square of grass that it is, now shrouded in wet, wintry darkness.

I slip in my earbuds and press play on the podcast about how homesteading changed someone's life. For the first twenty minutes, I am practically ebullient with relief, because the reasons why home-steading changed this person's life do not resonate with me at *all*. Josh joked about how he's not much of a prepper, but I'm even less so. I'm the *anti*-prepper because I have always maintained that I would rather choose not to survive in a world where I have to be worried about these things.

And so I have neither food security concerns nor goals. I am not thinking about 'preparedness' as a concept in the event of a global natural disaster or nuclear war, and I'm not interested in arming my-self for such a thing, either. And while I care about the environment, recycling as well as using paper straws and reusable shopping bags feels like enough of a contribution on my part to saving the planet.

If these are the reasons to homestead—in fact, the very *pillars* of the homesteading life, according to this podcast—then I am not a candidate, no matter what shadowy doubts have been whispering through my mind.

Phew!

Thank goodness, I think as I press pause on the podcast. I let Josh's usual energy and excitement start to carry me away, and I began to think that maybe there was something to this doing-something-different notion, but obviously there isn't, and I can go back to my original plan of convincing Josh—gently—that we are not doing this *Homesteading Thing*.

"What are you watching?"

My son's curious voice has me startling in my curled-up position. While I was deep in thought, Jack crept up to me, looking over my shoulder at the photo of my homesteading podcaster, a fortyish woman named Liz Simons who lives in rural Oregon and is pictured standing by a barn, one hand catching a beam, her hair in thick auburn braids as she smiles for the camera.

"Oh, I was just listening to a podcast," I say as dismissively as I can. It is never, ever a good idea to involve the children in these wild-eyed plans, especially when I am intending for said plans to die a swift, silent death. I slip my earbuds out of my ears as I smile at Jack in a let's-talk-about-something-else kind of way.

"A podcast about homesteading?" he asks, reading the heading as he leans forward to study the description of the podcast. There is an eager interest to his voice that makes me wilt inside because just like his dad, he's not going to let this go. Sure enough, his next eager question is, "Are we going to homestead? That would be so *cool*."

He really is his father's son.

"No, we are not going to homestead," I tell Jack firmly. "I was just listening to it out of interest, but it is definitely *not* the life for us. We are very happy right where we are, and we do not need to homestead in any way, shape, or form."

I spoke more forcefully than I needed to, just to drive the point home, and it's as I've finished this dire and determined pronouncement that I look up and see Josh standing in the doorway, still holding his briefcase, rain dampening the shoulders of his coat, his expression one of wounded disappointment.

We don't talk about that moment until we're getting ready for bed. There wasn't really an opportunity amidst all the chaos I keep telling myself is normal and happy—Rose came down from bed to hurl herself into Josh's arms and then insist she was hungry; William had to lament to him extensively about missing chess club; Jack jumped up and down and proclaimed that he "definitely, *definitely* had ADHD" and from the kitchen table Bethany shrieked at us all once again to be quiet.

"Mom," she pleaded, clearly thinking a direct appeal was needed, "this essay is super important. *Please.*"

"I know, I know." As a mother, I fall into a familiar routine of placating, then chastising, and hopefully guiding. "But you do have a desk in your room, Bethany. You could study there, and it would be a lot quieter for you."

"Well, I *thought* you might have wanted my company," she proclaimed in tearful aggravation, before gathering all her papers and books and huffily moving to the family room that adjoins the kitchen, where I already know the noise will be of equal irritation to her.

"Sounds like a lot's been going on," Josh remarked. He smiled at

Jack, Rose hoisted up on one hip, but his tone was a touch cool, and I knew that was for my benefit. He was hurt, and I couldn't blame him. I shouldn't have shut the homesteading thing down so derisively, but I didn't know he was listening.

But maybe that wasn't the point.

In any case, it's not until we're getting ready for bed that Josh mentions it. "How did homesteading come up with Jack?" he asks in a carefully neutral voice. "I thought we weren't going to mention anything to the kids at this juncture."

I was the one who had insisted we keep this between ourselves for now, although I really meant forever. Now, as I climb into bed, I sigh. "I was listening to a podcast and he saw it and jumped to conclusions." The right ones, as it happened, at least according to my husband.

"You were listening to a podcast?" Interest, as well as certain satisfied amusement, is audible in my husband's voice, and improbably, I find myself smiling.

"Don't get your hopes up," I warn him, still smiling. "You heard what I said to him."

"I think," Josh remarks archly, his eyes glinting with humor, "the lady doth protest too much."

"I admit," I feel compelled to confess, "I *have* been thinking about it. But that podcast actually made me realize it isn't for me, Josh."

If I expect Josh to feel disheartened by this admission, he isn't. He just cocks his head, his eyes alight, like he's ready to prove me wrong, which he probably is. "So why not?"

"We're not preppers," I state firmly. "And the four pillars of modern homesteading seem to be all about preparing for an eventual Armageddon. Food security. Sustainability. *Preparedness...*"

"None of those are bad things," Josh points out, all too reasonably.

"I know, but I don't actually *care* about them," I tell him with an earnestness of my own. "I mean, not *that* much. Not enough. If the world is in such a terrible state that we need to make all our own food... well, I don't want to live in that world." It sounds so obvious to me, but Josh frowns.

"Do you want your children to live in that world?" he asks seriously. "Do you want them to have the *chance* to live in that world?"

I fall silent.

"How about we do this," Josh suggests coaxingly. "How about we watch some videos together? There are some great homesteading YouTubers out there, as well as some online courses you can take—Homesteading 101 is a website that offers tons of online courses on just about every aspect of homesteading, and for just thirty bucks a month."

"You sound like a commercial," I tease. "Do you get a commission?"

He gives a small smile of acknowledgement, and I sigh, because I already know I'm going to say yes. Fine, I can watch a few videos, and maybe doing so will show Josh that we really aren't cut out for this lifestyle, no matter how frenetic modern life is, or dark and chaotic the world.

"I'll do that," I tell him, "Because you really seem to want me to give this a fair shake. But Josh..." I gentle my voice. "You know we can dislike aspects of modern life, of technology and politics and culture and all the rest, and *not* move to West Virginia or wherever to homestead? I mean... we can find a way to live in *this* world, in suburban New Jersey, that works for us." He doesn't respond and I press, "That's a real possibility, right?"

"Right," he replies, smiling, and I have a sinking feeling that neither of us believe what he's saying.

Chapter Six

Over the next six weeks, Josh and I watch countless videos on homesteading. I was game at first simply because this seemed a harmless if time-consuming way to scratch that particular itch he'd been feeling—that is, to do something different. We didn't have to *move* to satisfy him; we just needed to watch other people battling unruly goats, broken wells, and heavy clay soil that made it difficult to grow anything.

At some point, maybe two weeks in, my attitude shifted from sitting through these videos while tapping my foot, one eye on the clock, wondering when I'd be able to do something else, to actually feeling interested and even invested in what I was watching. We stumbled on the YouTube channel of a homesteader called Jane Do, a play on the term Jane Doe, named so because she could do just about anything. She and her husband had moved from their corporate jobs in Los Angeles to rural Virginia right after Covid, to homestead twenty acres and attempt to be mostly self-sufficient.

Jane is a woman around my age, but far fitter, with curly gray hair, a tanned and weathered face, and a personable and briskly practical demeanor. She talks through each skill she teaches on the YouTube video—from milking a cow to building a chicken coop to creating a hydroponic greenhouse, something I hadn't even known existed.

Unlike a lot of videos on YouTube, she doesn't make it look easy but films her mistakes, the way she learned, and finally how she succeeded. She has a wonderful ability to laugh at herself *and* get things done, and by the end of an episode, I feel—almost—like I could build a chicken coop or irrigate a garden or milk a goat myself. Jane has a way of making what clearly has to be back-breaking work look not necessarily easy, but purposeful and fun.

It was almost impossible to watch Jane moving briskly about her farm, cracking jokes for the camera, inviting us into her busy, productive life, and *not* yearn for something like it for ourselves. Josh joked I had a girl crush on Jane, and I kind of did. She was the type of person I aspired to be—capable but also real, acknowledging her failures and yet forging on. We clocked a *lot* of hours watching Jane Do homestead. I knew Josh was hoping this would be the catalyst that had me leaping onto the other side of the argument, both feet in, but in truth, watching her was like watching any good TV show. I enjoyed it the way I would a story, becoming immersed in all the details and descriptions of her interesting life, and when it was over I moved on to *my* life, which was nothing like hers, and that was fine by me. Mostly.

If we'd stuck with Jane Do, I'm not sure we would have got much farther in our *homesteading journey*, which was what Josh had started calling it, even though I kept laughingly (but also seriously) reminding him that we weren't going anywhere. I could put Jane Do in a mental box of escapist entertainment and forget about her.

But then we stumbled upon the Walker family. We have the 'What to Watch Next' suggestion to blame for that. It was so easy to click on the link and start watching, as we idly wondered who the Walkers were... and then, within one video, got completely sucked into their family life.

The Walkers are a family with six kids who traded life in urban Washington DC for thirty acres in Tennessee. The father Jay had been in the military police, the mom Sarah a part-time data analyst. They chucked their jobs in and moved to their homestead with about as much experience as we had, learning on the job, and documenting it for posterity as well as their seventy thousand YouTube subscribers.

There was something so real and warm about them; they had none of the glossy mirage of perfection that I saw so often on social media, although their life certainly did look appealing—the big farmhouse kitchen that moved seamlessly into a living room with a huge stone fireplace, the whole space wood-beamed and comfortably cluttered, with plenty of hand-crocheted blankets tossed around, a pot of something delicious always simmering on the stove.

We watched Sarah teach her two youngest daughters, just five and seven years old, how to make jam. We were rapt as Jay and their oldest son, seventeen-year-old Elijah, helped to birth a calf and then wept together when it died. We cheered—actually out loud—when thirteen-year-old Ruth ventured into the apiary for the first time to collect honey, despite a deep phobia of bees. It was gripping stuff, like *Little House on the Prairie*, but modern and real and relevant, even to Josh and me, who were trying to parent our own kids, minus the apiary, the cows, the chickens. So many life lessons could be learned, I came to realize, on a farm. Life lessons we were struggling to teach our children in suburban New Jersey.

I suppose it was inevitable that the kids would get in on it all. Josh and I had been watching the videos upstairs in our bedroom, with the door closed, so they wouldn't cotton on to any wild ideas

I was still very much not on board with. We couldn't, however, disappear for an hour every evening without someone noticing, and sure enough, while we were both raptly watching Jay coach ten-year-old Samuel on how to shoot his first deer, William came into our bedroom.

"What are you guys *doing*?"

We both startled guiltily, slamming down the lid of Joshua's laptop like we'd been caught watching porn, or maybe just an R-rated movie, which we didn't normally allow.

"Umm..." My mind was blank.

"William," Josh rebuked him, "you're meant to knock."

"I did. *Twice*." William stepped closer to us. "Was that a kid with a *gun*?"

He sounded anxious, and so Josh sought to reassure him. "His dad was teaching him how to shoot a deer."

William did not look mollified. "Why were you watching that?"

"Well..." Josh glanced at me, as if asking for permission to share about the whole *Homesteading Thing*. I didn't give it. "It was just interesting," he finished lamely.

William did not look at all convinced, and then Jack, always ready to go where the action is, catapulted into our bedroom. "What are you guys doing?" He spied the laptop on the bed. "Hey, Mom, are you listening to more of that homesteading stuff?"

"Homesteading stuff?" William repeated, sounding alarmed. "*What*?"

At that point, it had been three weeks since Jack had stumbled upon me listening to that podcast. This was a kid who couldn't remember where he put his sneakers five minutes ago, yet he remembered *that*?

"It's interesting, William," Josh said. He didn't look at me as he lifted the screen of the laptop. "Have a look."

Within thirty seconds, both William and Jack were mesmerized. It was inevitable that Bethany would come upstairs, in a slight huff because she'd been abandoned alone in the family room, although at least she'd had her precious quiet. By that point, we'd moved onto another video of the Walkers all making homemade Christmas presents for each other, to a background of roaring log fires and snow blanketing the Great Smoky Mountains, Christmas carols around a battered piano and gingerbread cookies straight out of the oven.

Who wouldn't be both charmed and enthralled by such a scene, by such a *life*?

Rose, hearing the commotion, got out of bed—not as rare an occurrence as I would like—and scrambled into ours, squashing herself right between Josh and me. Before long, all six of us were piled onto our bed like something out of a children's story, watching Walker videos until eleven o'clock at night.

And they all had *school* the next day. I don't know what we were thinking, but from that point on we binged on the Walker videos nearly every night, watching them in our bed because somehow that had become a tradition that the kids insisted on, with us all squashed in there together.

As reluctant as I still was about this whole venture, I did treasure those evenings, my arm snugged around Rose, Jack leaning into my shoulder, Bethany perched by Josh and William on the edge of the bed, his arms folded and his lips pursed like he wasn't convinced by this beautiful family, and yet he was as entranced as we were.

The comments everyone made were the best part. Somehow, through watching the Walkers learn on the job, we all became self-declared experts on everything.

"That greenhouse looks way too small," Bethany stated definitively, as we watched them repurpose old windows and birch logs to make a no-cost structure. "It needs more light, too, if they're going to grow anything."

"There's a reason why they're called chokeberries," Jack snorted when a jam-making recipe went wrong, and resulted in six jars of bitter, inedible stuff.

"I think they're spending way too much money on machinery," William announced when Jay Walker shared their budget, explaining the breakdown. "They'd be better off investing in livestock. Far better value."

Rose glanced up at me, her face alight. "Can we live like that?" she asked simply, eyes shining with hope and wonder. We'd just watched an episode where the Walkers' barn cat Phoebe had given birth to six tiny, perfect kittens. They looked like little balls of gray cashmere. Rose, who had been asking for a cat for over a year, had been utterly enthralled. "It's a nice way to live," I remarked neutrally. I tried not to meet Josh's gaze, but somehow I had to, and I saw the same question in his eyes. *Can we live like that*?

I looked away.

As nice as those evenings were, and as entertaining and heartwarming the videos, still none of it seems to me to be a reason to upend our lives, which I tell Josh whenever the topic comes up, which is surprisingly not that often. I suspect he is biding his time, waiting for me to come round, but I'm just not.

"I mean, how would it even *work*," I ask him abruptly, before he's even said anything to me, one evening in late March when the kids have gone to bed, and we are still in the kitchen. I am emptying the third dishwasher cycle of the day and Josh is putting Max to bed with a biscuit and his favorite toy.

Outside the sky is hazed with red from all the traffic lights in our neighborhood, and in the distance I hear the squeal of brakes and the sound of a siren. We don't live in the inner city by any means, but our neighboring town to Princeton is staunchly suburban. And I'm *noticing* it more.

I suppose it would be hard not to, when we've been spending several hours a day watching a family enjoy the rustic beauty of rural Tennessee. The last episode we watched had them stargazing all together, wrapped in homemade woolen blankets and lying on the flat roof of one of their barns, pointing out constellations to each other as they sipped hot chocolate from a thermos.

Slowly Josh straightens. "We'd take it day by day," he replies, and I shake my head, impatient not with him, but with myself. Why am I even asking this?

"I'm not talking truisms," I tell him. "I mean seriously. How would we homeschool Bethany, who is taking five AP classes right now? How would William play chess? And how would we manage all the actual homesteading stuff? I've never grown anything besides some houseplants. You haven't built anything bigger than a book-case." And even that was wobbly, consigned to the basement to store old bike helmets. "And what about our family and friends?" I add. "We just leave them—everyone—to go to a place where we don't know a single soul?"

Josh is silent for a moment, his face drawn into a thoughtful frown. "Are these serious questions?" he finally asks.

"I don't know," I admit, and then amend, "Not really."

Josh slowly nods. "Okay, then let's just keep learning," he suggests after a moment. Max is curled up in his bed, and I've finished un-loading the dishwasher. All around us the kitchen stretches, quiet and dark, messy and modern, without any of the cozy homeliness of the Walker kitchen. Not, I tell myself sternly, that I am comparing myself or my kitchen to them or theirs… and yet, of course I am.

"I signed up for the Homesteading 101 site," Josh tells me. "The one with all the courses. I thought we could watch some of them. As much as I love the Walkers, I don't want their life. I want ours."

"Their life is pretty amazing," I admit grudgingly, and Josh smiles. "Ours could be too."

The implication seems obvious—that it isn't now. And as much as I do like our life—because I *do*—I can't help but agree. I think of the snarl of traffic on Route 1, the endless carpooling and laundry, the constant monitoring of screens, the way we sometimes seem like a family of disparate parts rather than a cohesive, supportive unit… the way the Walkers are.

I really am comparing myself to them, but maybe that's not a bad thing. It gives us something to aspire to, anyway. Josh said the life we have now isn't working, and I am starting to agree with him. I've been living with constant levels of aggravation, hassle and discontentedness without even realizing I was doing so. But would I have those same levels, albeit in a different way, in West Virginia or wherever we decided to homestead?

From all the videos we've watched, homesteading is *way* more work than living in the suburbs where you buy your food prepack-aged from ShopRite, you can hire someone to mow your lawn, and the only animal you have is a dog—and maybe a cat if Rose ever gets her way. Why are we talking like homesteading will somehow be *easier*?

Or is it that our lives are *too* easy now, and that's part of the problem?

"What course were you thinking?" I ask.

"There's an introduction to homesteading class that covers the basics, how to get started. It might be interesting, regardless of what we end up doing."

I hesitate, feeling as if I'm edging out to a precipice, half out of desire, half not by my own will. Why am I even thinking about this? It's not like we're actually going to move anywhere... right?

"All right," I relent, in part because I am curious, in part to appease Josh, and also in part because I would really like to be more like Sarah Walker or Jane Do.

Josh grins, his eyes sparkling. "Great."

It's nearly eleven o'clock at night, and we both have to be up early. I head over to the kitchen counter to charge my phone and groan out loud at the snarl of charging cables that are there, none of which have the right connector, which is just so *typical*.

If we lived on a homestead, I think with a savage twist of humor, *we wouldn't have these cords. Maybe we wouldn't even have phones.*

I'm not sure why I think this; the older Walker kids have phones. It's not like homesteading means you suddenly become Amish.

I finally find the right cord and plug in my phone, only to discover the cord, a cheap knockoff, doesn't work. Another groan bursts out of me, closer to a howl of rage.

Josh, without saying a word, calmly hands me another cable, one that works.

As I plug it in, I mutter my thanks, shaking my head, half-wishing I didn't even have a phone.

"Don't say a word," I warn Josh, and he just smiles before he pulls me in for a hug.

"I won't," he promises, but he basically already did.

Chapter Seven

In April, spring bursts onto the scene like the heroine of a romance novel, blowsy and dreamy and heartstoppingly beautiful, and this season I seem to notice it more. I marvel at the pink puffballs of cherry blossoms as I drive William to chess club. "That tree is *entirely* pink," I say with a laugh of pure wonder. I crouch down in our front yard and cup my hands around the tiny crocuses pushing themselves up determinedly from the damp grass; I crumble soil beneath my fingers and notice how loose it is, which means it's good for growing. It's no wonder New Jersey is called the Garden State.

All those hours of videos have made me a pseudo-expert; I am still sane enough to realize I have no real knowledge, but I definitely have an awareness, and that is affecting both my outlook and my life.

I also feel the need to *do* something. Something productive and tangible and real. I buy some glass jars with hinged lids and decant all my store-bought pasta and rice into them, simply because they look so pleasingly homemade on my pantry shelf. I survey our quarter acre backyard and consider what I could do with that space. I start taking a weird kind of pleasure in things I once found mundane and irritating—folding laundry, stirring soup, walking Max.

I'm happier, I realize, and Josh does too, because one evening as I'm kneading bread—I *know*—he catches me around the waist.

"Well, hello Abby Do," he teases, and I swat him away, laughing but also a little alarmed. All right, I might be making some small changes to my life, but that doesn't *mean* anything. I still have to believe that.

"This is me showing you that the homesteading life you want is possible here," I tell him pointedly. "In some measure, anyway." Josh raises his hands in mock surrender.

"Sure. Okay."

We've been taking the Homesteading 101 course online, an hour a week, most of it about dreams and goals and what you want to get out of the homesteading experience. "Knowing your why" is a big part of it, and that's the thing I can't yet articulate—or believe in. And so we decided to press pause on the course until we could talk more about it, but with the usual busyness of life we haven't yet, and maybe that's just as well. These baby steps are enough for me.

But they're not enough for Josh. One evening as I'm ready to go out for my bimonthly book club—something I dread but usually end up enjoying—I come across him browsing plots of lands in Virginia on a real estate website and let out a snort of disbelief.

"So now, in addition to homesteading and homeschooling, we're going to build our own house?"

"It could be cheaper," Josh replies, refusing to rise to my slightly sneering tone, which makes me feel petty. That kind of scornful incredulity is starting to feel like my only defense, and it's not a very good one. He lowers the lid of his laptop as he gives me an unsettlingly compassionate gaze. "I'm not trying to rush ahead or force anything, Abby. I just want to see what's out there."

I nod, wanting to feel appeased, but the truth is I don't. Already it feels like this situation is slipping out of my control; we've spent more time exploring homesteading than we have any of Josh's other wild ideas. That is both exciting and worrying, and the fact that it's both is most worrying of all.

"I have my book club," I tell him as I button my coat. "But we can talk about this later."

He nods, affable as ever. "Okay. Enjoy. What worthy tome have you read this time?"

I just shrug, because I can't remember the name of it and the truth is, I haven't read it. We always pick some modern classic that I find either too dense or esoteric to read, but I still plow through a couple of chapters, with the best of intentions.

Now, as I drive to my friend Kerry's house to discuss the book whose title I can't remember, I feel a wave of anxiety roll through me. I'm not even sure what I'm anxious about—the possibility of a major life change or the far more likely possibility that it *won't* happen. If this homesteading thing peters out over the summer, as it is surely likely to do, will I feel disappointed or relieved or both?

Both, I realize, and that feels like a lose-lose proposition. I've come to the uncomfortable realization that I wasn't happy before Josh mentioned it to me, but I'd thought I was. Isn't that almost as good?

A groan escapes me, and I shake my head. I have spent so much emotional energy thinking about this. For one evening, I want to think about something else, even if it's just a book I haven't read.

But when I arrive at my friend Kerry's house, I can already feel that I'm not in the mood. The book club was formed back when Bethany was in elementary school, and I've drifted from the other moms as their kids have gone to different schools, they've gone back to work, and life has just moved on. I don't see any of them except Kerry outside of this club, and as I come into her sprawling modern kitchen and glimpse the knot of women sipping wine by the granite island, I am very conscious of that fact. I know at least three of them see each other regularly—Pilates class, a couples' supper club, power walking through the park, the middle-aged mom version of a playdate.

"*Abby.*" Kerry air-kisses me on both cheeks before she ushers me forward. "How are you? I feel like I haven't seen you in ages."

She hasn't, and I smile and murmur some kind of acknowledgement. Kerry's daughter Isabel was Bethany's best friend all through elementary school, but then in middle school they parted company in a particularly brutal way. Two days before the start of seventh grade, Isabel informed Bethany straight up that she was planning to be popular in junior high, and so she couldn't be friends with brainy Bethany anymore. It was the kind of savage power play that was reminiscent of a medieval court more than a middle school, but maybe there's not that much difference between those two worlds. In any case, Isabel went on her quest for popularity and managed to elevate her social position somewhat, while Bethany, quietly devastated, doubled down on her academics and made best friends with Amelia Lee, a South Korean girl who was as driven as she was.

My friendship with Kerry became strained as a result, and there were a couple of years where we hardly saw each other at all, and I dropped out of the book club because I felt like I had to. It felt like Kerry was giving me the Isabel treatment, but at the end of eighth grade Isabel had a fallout with her friendship group, came whimpering back to Bethany, and Kerry invited the whole family over for a Memorial Day barbecue. I tried not to be cynical about it, and then when the girls went to different high schools we resumed our occasional coffees together, and I rejoined this book club.

Two years on, I'm not all that sure why I did, only that I felt a compulsion to do something social, not out of a fear of missing out but more a fear of *seeming* like I was missing out. What that says about me I'm not sure I want to consider.

Lindsay, one of the moms I really don't know all that well, turns to me, elegant eyebrows raised. "Abby," she says by way of greeting. "I feel like I haven't seen you in forever. How have you been? How's the family?"

"Oh, we're..." For some reason I stop, and all five women turn to look at me expectantly. I see a flash of something in Lindsay's eyes, and I'm afraid it's a sort of gleeful anticipation that I'm going to say we're struggling. *Schadenfreude* is a real thing, especially among middle-aged mothers. "We're fine," I finish, and it feels as if a collective breath has been exhaled from the group.

"That's great," Lindsay gushes, like I've said something profound. "Life is so busy, isn't it? This time of year..." She shakes her head. "We're all waiting for summer, but then summer is so busy too, isn't it? Ryan is doing the engineering program at The Governor's School... Did I tell you?"

No, of course she didn't tell me; I haven't seen her in months and the acceptances were only given out at the end of March. The Governor's School is one of the most competitive summer programs for high school juniors in the whole state; Bethany applied for a place on the chemistry program and wasn't accepted. I wonder if Lindsay knows that. All the applicants went to a reception a couple of weeks ago; Bethany didn't mention seeing Ryan.

"That's amazing," I say to Lindsay. "Tell him congratulations for me."

"I will," Lindsay assures me. "What's Bethany doing this summer?" The question is phrased so innocently, eyes rounded, mouth a lipsticked *o,* that I am sure she knew Bethany didn't get accepted, and I wonder why on earth I am playing this game.

"She's working at our local ShopRite," I tell her. "And doing an internship at Parker Pharmaceuticals."

Which is perfectly *fine,* great even, but Bethany was bitterly disappointed that she didn't get accepted to the Governor program, and I can tell by the look on Lindsay's face that I might as well have said that my daughter has just dropped out of high school. Suddenly I feel like I can't stand another minute of this snobbish fakery, and so I turn to Kerry.

"What did you think of the book?" I ask her brightly, which is probably not the smartest question since I didn't read it. Fortunately, though, I can nod and smile along as she gives her opinion, and the conversation moves on. I sip my wine and let it flow over me, wishing I could shake my low mood, but I can't.

I am quiet throughout the whole evening as my friends talk about the book a little but mostly chat and gossip as the wine flows and Kerry passes around a platter of cut-up carrot and celery sticks with some low-fat hummus. I watch Denise nibble a carrot stick as Laura pontificates about the book's themes of identity and culture and I let myself drift.

I used to feel like I belonged here. The occasional, wide-eyed, catty remark would have annoyed me a little, yes, but now *everything* grates. I'm not sure I even like these women, but maybe that's more about me than them. My threshold for all the things that I used to put up with has become alarmingly low.

"Abby, are you okay?" Kerry asks with a concerned smile, after about an hour of discussion. "You've been so quiet tonight."

"Yes, Abby, what's going on with you?" Denise asks. "In your life, I mean, besides the usual runaround?" Her smile is warm, but her eyes are shrewd as she and everyone else waits for me to dish some dirt about my life. They all want to hear it, I know.

"Well..." I pause and glance around the room. I'm about to launch into the usual spiel about work and school and yes, the usual runaround, when something else comes out of my mouth instead. "Actually, we've been thinking about moving to West Virginia to homestead."

Chapter Eight

The silence that greets my statement is total. Five women stare at me, utterly gobsmacked and frankly horrified. Then Lindsay slowly shakes her head.

"I'm sorry, *what?*"

"Homestead," I repeat, enunciating clearly because even though I've immersed myself in the world of greenhouses and chicken coops, permaculture and hydroponics, these women have not. The word *homestead* has probably not crossed their lips or their minds in decades, if ever.

"Abby!" Kerry sounds half-scolding, half-laughing, like she's not sure if I've told a joke, but if I have, I need to know it wasn't a funny one. "What on earth are you talking about?"

"I know, it sounded crazy to me too, at first," I tell her with a smile. I find I am perversely enjoying their complete stupefaction. "I mean, *totally* crazy. But Josh and I have been researching that whole world and honestly, it seems like a really healthy and happy way to live, especially as a family."

"So this is one of Josh's wild ideas," Kerry clarifies, and for a second I cringe because her playfully sneering tone is the same kind I use when talking about my husband's schemes. The only reason she's talking about Josh's wild ideas is because I've told her about them.

"It was," I agree carefully, "but we're all getting on board now, even the kids." At least they are in theory. But watching YouTube videos is a far cry from living that life ourselves... as I've pointed out to Josh many times.

Lindsay lets out an incredulous laugh. She's enjoying this too, I realize, and I know I have most likely provided fodder for the gossip mill for weeks. *You'll never guess what Abby Bryant is thinking about doing...* "Are you for real?" she demands. "I mean, what on earth, Abby? Are you going to, like, *churn butter*?" She lets out another laugh, glancing at the other women as if inviting them to share the joke... which is me.

I feel my cheeks warm. "Maybe," I reply recklessly. "We're just looking into our options now. We're taking a homesteading course online to learn how to go about it."

"A *course*?" Denise repeats, wrinkling her nose. "I had no idea they even existed."

"I didn't either," I tell her, smiling, but she just looks away.

I feel like I've become either a joke or a pariah, maybe both. I am not following the script of our conversations, of our lives, and that understandably makes them uncomfortable. It would have made *me* uncomfortable, if I'd been on the other side of this chasm—and it *is* a chasm, because I already know my friends are never going to understand why I am even considering this at all, never mind seriously, which I now realize I am. And I feel too tired and overwhelmed to attempt to explain it to them, or even to myself.

"Well, it's just something we're thinking about," I say, with an air of finality, and I feel their palpable sense of relief that I've let it go. We go back to talking about the book, and I even make a few remarks based on the summary I read of it online. By ten o'clock, the mood is winding down, and I decide to say my goodbyes.

After the usual flurry of 'so nice to see you's, Kerry accompanies me to the door. "Abby... this homesteading thing... it's not serious, is it?" she asks, sounding genuinely concerned. "I mean, I know Josh has his crazy ideas, and you humor him, but..." She trails off, waiting for me to fill in the blanks with the obvious reassurances.

"He does, and this was one of them," I agree as I zip up my coat. "But this feels different to me." I pause to look at her squarely. "Kerry... don't you ever feel like you want something more out of life? That you want to switch it up, do something different, startle yourself out of sleepwalking through your days?" I sound like Josh; my voice has the same earnest intensity.

"Whoa." Kerry holds up a hand to forestall me from saying anything more. "Yes, okay, I mean, everyone feels that way sometimes. But Abby..." She shakes her head. "Come *on*. The solution is to get a new haircut, or go on vacation, or I don't know... find a hobby."

It's more or less what I have said to Josh on more than one occasion. "Yeah," I agree after a moment. "Yeah, that makes sense."

A smile of relief breaks across her face. "Okay, so no more talk about moving to West Virginia, okay? I'd miss you too much." She gives me a quick hug, and I don't point out that before tonight, I hadn't actually seen Kerry in three months. And I haven't seen her outside of book club for over a year. Truthfully? I don't think she'd miss me much at all.

We say goodbye and I step out into the cool spring evening. The air is fresh and damp with a hint of chill, and in the hazy, orange glow of the sodium streetlights I get into my car. I let my mind empty out as I drive the twenty minutes back home, but halfway there, on

Route 518, I suddenly pull over onto the shoulder by a stretch of farmland, the sky endlessly black and crystalline-clear, scattered with a few glittering pinpoints of stars. For a second I simply take in the view, let it restore me as the unsettledness I felt all evening begins to dissipate.

Realistically and reasonably, I know a subpar book club group is not a reason to move, just as watching YouTube videos isn't a reason, or the traffic on Route 1, or the fact that William doesn't have any friends and Jack needs more activity and Bethany is so stressed and Rose still doesn't know how to tie her shoes. None of these are reasons, really, and yet...

They *all* are. And more than that... or at least in addition to it, is the seam of restlessness running right through me, the belief that life is—or maybe the fear that it isn't—more than trudging through Costco or scrolling through Netflix looking for something mindless to watch, or waiting in an endless carpool line, already ten minutes late for the next activity.

I breathe in and out deeply as I stare at the sky. Then I pull back onto the road and I drive the rest of the way home.

The kids are in bed and Josh is on the family room sofa, his laptop perched on his knees, as I come into the kitchen. Max looks up from his bed and then lets his head droop back onto his paws.

"Hey, how was it?" he asks as I drop my car keys into the little dish with a clang.

"Oh, the same," I reply. "I don't know why I bother going, when I hardly ever read the book." I shrug as I come to sit beside him on the sofa. "Let me guess. You've spent the whole evening watching YouTube videos on how to plan out your five acres for maximum food production and security."

"I call it doing research," Josh corrects me with a smile, and I tip my head back against the sofa and close my eyes.

"I told Kerry and the other women at the book club that we're thinking of homesteading."

"You did?" Josh sounds understandably surprised, as well as a little amused. "What was their reaction?"

I let out a soft huff of laughter. "About what you'd imagine."

"So what yours was, back at the beginning?" His voice is full of affection and a ghost of a smile touches my lips.

"I guess so."

Josh rests one hand on my shoulder; the weight is comforting, and I lean into him a little. "You okay, Abs?" he asks gently.

"Yes. Sort of. I don't know." I sigh, a gust of sound. "I'm seriously thinking about this whole homesteading thing now, and that scares me. A lot." Josh doesn't reply and eventually I open my eyes. He is staring at me thoughtfully, a frown line furrowing his brow, his lips slightly pursed. "What?" I ask him.

"Why does it scare you?" he asks seriously.

"Because we *never* do your crazy ideas," I burst out. "And I don't want to move to West Virginia and then realize I actually hate everything about it. I don't want to find out that I hate keeping chickens or having a vegetable garden or... *churning butter*. And as for homeschooling... I *like* having the kids in school. Six or seven hours of peace and quiet is pretty darned good. And what about our friends?" Even if I more or less dismissed them all moments ago. "Or my dad, or your parents... besides, I *like* going to Target and having takeout and general suburban life," I continue, even though there are definite parts of that life that I really don't. "I like things being convenient. I like having neighbors." Even if we don't actually know the names of ours, who moved in three years ago. I like neighbors as a *concept*. "But most of all," I finish, "what if we hate it, Josh? What if this is just the kind of stupid thing you dream about but never do? What if it's *meant* to be that? You know there are dreams that are just meant to stay dreams. Maybe this is that. And if we actually go for it and it all blows up... then what?" I fall silent as I collapse against the sofa, having expended all my energy, both mental and physical, on my panicked diatribe.

Josh is unfazed by my outburst; he is quiet, clearly thinking. "Okay, let's go point by point," he finally says. "West Virginia, or wherever we might choose to move, is not Mars. We can still go to Target and get takeout, but we might have to drive a little farther, that's all. We'll see family. West Virginia is actually closer to my parents in Maryland, you know, and your dad would love to visit us if we were homesteading. You know how much he loves his little patio garden. As for friends..." He pauses. "Not to be harsh or anything, but we just don't *see* our friends that much anymore. Which is one of the things I don't like about general suburban life. Everyone is so busy with the mundane necessities of life here... if we lived in a place where there was more community, where everyone helped each other out... I feel like that would be so much better for all of us."

"There's no guarantee of that happening," I point out. "Wherever we move. It's not like West Virginia has cornered the market on neighborliness."

"No," he agrees, "but in the homesteading world, people seem to rely on each other more. They know they need each other's help to get by." I think of the Walker videos; it did seem like someone was stopping by or coming through their homestead just about every day, to lend a hand or ask for advice or just say hello. But are the

Walkers even *real*?

Maybe they live in a McMansion in Nashville and that whole homesteading life of theirs is fake, like so much on the internet is. "Everyone's so busy here," Josh continues, "and we lose touch, and a year goes by without any contact. I feel like moving wouldn't affect our friendships as much as you might think it would."

Which is depressing as well as probably true.

"As for the rest... if we discover we don't like it..." Josh scratches his chin. "That's a fair point," he concedes. "And I've been thinking along the same lines myself. So, how about this? We start home-steading now, here, as best as we can, and see how it goes? At the end of the summer, we can re-evaluate."

I stare at him in surprise. It's a sensible idea, and yet... "How would we even do that?"

Josh shrugs. "We make a vegetable garden in the backyard. We build a greenhouse. We keep chickens. We put down our phones as often as we can, and we take the kids off screens, too. We try to live more slowly and sustainably here, to see if we can do it somewhere else."

"I'm not sure we're even legally allowed to keep chickens in New Jersey," I point out. "There are all these regulations about distance from residences and coop size and stuff like that. I don't think we have enough space."

He arches an eyebrow, a smile lurking about his mouth. "How do you know that?"

I duck my head. "I might have already looked it up online."

Josh lets out a shout of laughter and then wraps his arm around me, pulling me into his shoulder. "I love it," he says as I press my cheek against his chest. "I love you."

"I love you, too."

He presses a kiss to the top of my head. "Let's just do as much as we can and feel like we want to do, okay? And see if we like it? Because you're right. We don't want to move somewhere and invest all this time and energy into something that ends up not being actually for us."

"Okay..." I say slowly. I realize I feel excited about the thought of doing something *now*, rather than chasing hazy dreams for a future that I still think is most likely *not* going to happen. No more watching the Walkers live their idyllic life in Tennessee, whether it's fake or not. The Bryants are going to live *their* life in New Jersey.

Whatever that looks like.

"So what will it look like?" I ask Josh.

He laughs and kisses my head again. "Whatever we want it to."

Chapter Nine

The next morning Josh makes his famous (at least in our family) blueberry pancakes, and we get the kids up by nine o'clock to have a Family Meeting, with capital letters.

"What's going on?" Bethany asks, her tone caught between complaint and curiosity, as she stumbles into the kitchen, still in her pajamas and sporting a serious case of bedhead. The air wafts with the smell of frying bacon and fresh coffee, and spring sunshine pours through the French windows. It feels like a great time to be alive.

"We're having a Family Meeting!" Josh announces grandly as he flips a pancake three feet in the air. He is full of energy and optimism and watching him makes me smile. It also makes me realize how he *hasn't* been like this for a long time. Too long. He's been beaten down by the slog of suburban life just as I have.

"A family meeting?" Bethany sounds suspicious as she slouches into a chair at the table, already scrolling on her phone. "Why?"

"Because we have things to discuss," Josh replies. "Important things. Good things."

Both these statements only alarm Bethany, who straightens. "What kind of things?"

Before Josh can answer, and I'm as curious as Bethany as to how he would handle that one, Rose comes running into the kitchen, crying noisily as she barrels right into me, followed by a grinning Jack, who was clearly chasing her.

"Jack took off my covers," she sobs against my stomach. "And I was *asleep*!"

Jack gives me a look of round-eyed innocence. "You told me to wake her up."

"Gently," I remind him. I sit down at the table with my coffee and Rose on my lap. "I'm glad you're awake, sweetheart," I tell her, "because we're having an important family breakfast."

Rose peeks up at me, her lashes spangled with teardrops. "Important?"

"Why are we all getting up so early?" William asks as he comes into the kitchen. Like Bethany, he is in his pajamas, dark hair rumpled as he cleans his glasses with the corner of his t-shirt. "What's going on?"

"Everyone gather round for pancakes and we'll tell you," Josh says in the same grand voice he used before. "Hustle now!"

Slowly, with varying degrees of grumbling and curiosity, our four children gather around the table. Josh tells Bethany to put away her phone, and she rolls her eyes and huffs, but does it. William is already looking anxious, and Rose is still sniffing away the last of her tears. With a lurch of trepidation, I wonder if this is going to work at all. Yes, we all liked watching those YouTube videos, but doing it ourselves? The kids are never going to get on board. I'm not sure *I'm* on board, despite my initial enthusiasm. I've never really done any gardening, at least successfully, save for a couple of hydrangea bushes I planted when we first moved. Every spring I go to the garden center and haphazardly buy a few perennials that usually die by August. Even my houseplants struggle.

"So what is this oh-so important meeting?" Bethany asks with another eyeroll for good measure. "Because I need to study for the SAT next weekend." After scoring a very respectable 1400 on the SAT in February, Bethany wants to retake them to try for a higher score. Josh thought she shouldn't, because of the added stress, but she was adamant, as she has been about so many admirable things, and yet, like he said, they don't seem good for her. It always feels as if she's on the edge, and we keep trying to pull her back, to no avail.

"Mom and I have been talking," Josh says, and I am glad he's taking the lead. "We want to try to slow down a little, live life a bit more sustainably and intentionally."

Bethany rolls her eyes for a third time. I almost quip that if she does it again they might stay that way. "For heaven's sake, Dad," she says, "you sound like a teenaged girl's Instagram reel. *Intentionally?*"

"Wow, result," Josh replies with a grin, clearly unfazed. "That must mean I'm trendy."

This does not even earn an eyeroll from our oldest daughter. She just groans and shakes her head.

"Anyway," Josh continues, serious now, "we want to try this. Take a page out of the Walkers' book—"

"The *Walkers*?" William interrupts. "You mean, like on YouTube?" He sounds incredulous.

"Yes, on YouTube," Josh replies. "We were thinking of planting a vegetable garden in the backyard. Spending less time on screens and more time together, making things grow. And learning how to do some other stuff."

"Okaay." Bethany draws the word out as she stabs a piece of pancake. "And this required a major family meeting? You guys planting beans or something and you want us to scatter some seeds?"

"Well," Josh replies mildly, "we want everyone to be involved in a significant way. That's kind of the point."

"If we live like the Walkers," Rose asks eagerly, "can I get a cat?"

"If we move to a house like the Walkers," I reply, "you can get a cat."

Josh grins at me. "You might regret making that promise," he says, and I shrug, because I don't really think this is going to go much farther than us planting some tomatoes in the yard and probably watching them wither and die.

"Wait," William says slowly as he puts down his fork. "What do you mean, *moving*?"

Josh and I exchange the kind of parental glances that involve an entire conversation in a single look—*should we mention what we've been thinking of? Do we want to panic them? We've got to tell them at some point. But only if we're serious... But we are serious. I'm not sure we are.*

Josh turns to William. "Mom and I have talked about moving," he says. "Eventually. Maybe. One day."

"Moving where?" Jack asks. He sounds curious rather than worried.

"Somewhere with some land," Josh replies cautiously. "Where we could do this all properly, for real."

"You mean, *really* be like the Walkers?" Rose asks. She sounds thrilled.

"Well, we wouldn't be the Walkers," Josh tells her as he reaches over to ruffle her hair. "We'd be the Bryants, living the Bryants' lives. But sort of like that, yes."

"*What*—" The single word from Bethany is a screech.

"Cool," Jack breathes.

Rose squeals, and William says nothing, looking like he got the wind knocked right out of him.

"But right now," I interject hurriedly, "we're just talking about planting a garden here, in the backyard."

"Right," Josh says as he sits back in his chair with a canary-eating grin. "That's all we're talking about... now."

The next half hour is a tsunami of questions, some asked in strident tones, others in ones of growing excitement. Bethany moves from alarm to scornful disbelief and then back again, and William has gone very quiet. Rose has asked me three times about a cat. Jack asked if he could have an airsoft gun.

Josh fields all their questions with easy laughter—one of his greatest skills—while I sip my coffee and try not to panic. *We're crazy*, I think, *even to be thinking of this*, but the sentiment, which I've thought often enough, lacks the panicked conviction that has accompanied it in the past.

And somehow it doesn't *feel* crazy when Jack insists we should get started right away, and we all end up trooping out to the backyard still in our pajamas, and marking out a vegetable patch with a roll of twine William found in the kitchen junk drawer. Rose wants to plant one of the blueberries from her pancake, and I have to explain that you can't plant blueberries like seeds—although I'm not one hundred percent sure of that—and also we'll need to till the soil first... or something. I am really not an authority on any of these matters, which makes me think—again—that we must be crazy, and this time I believe it more.

Except then Josh says he can rent a tiller from the local garden center; he's already called, and he can pick it up this very morning. He tells the kids they can come with him, and everyone can choose some seeds or a plant for our brand new, as-yet-to-be-made vegetable garden.

Miraculously, even Bethany agrees to go, and feeling like I need to catch my breath, I offer to stay behind and tidy up our breakfast dishes while Josh takes all the kids out like it's Christmas and they're getting to pick out their presents.

As they pull out of the driveway, leaving me and Max in blissful quiet, I pour myself a cup of coffee and sink into a chair at the kitchen table. *We're just making a garden*, I tell myself, but it feels like so much more than that. I feel like I've just stepped on a train that's picking up speed with every breath I take, and I don't even remember getting on it.

And yet... despite Bethany's grumbles and William's shock, this morning has been one of the happiest I can remember in a long time. And we've spent more time together, as a family, than we have in months, with no one even *wanting* to be on a screen.

Maybe we don't need to move to West Virginia after all.

Or maybe we do.

I can't tell if this is the beginning of something big, or the end of something that was always going to be small. We plant the garden, this weird restlessness goes away, I get a new haircut like Kerry suggested, and we rent a house somewhere remote for a week and realize we're scared of the forest. And Josh's crazy homesteading idea becomes another family joke, on par with the Falkland Islands or the school bus life.

Why does that likelihood feel dispiriting rather than reassuring? Have I changed, or has the dream?

I finish my coffee and tidy up the kitchen, answer a text about bringing in cupcakes for a fundraiser for Rose's school—*please only bring store-bought baked goods, with a complete list of ingredients for any allergies, gluten and dairy-free options always welcome*!—check my email and see that I have four overdue library books, a nagging work email even though it's a Saturday, and it's time for Max's heart-worm treatment next week, *please book your appointment today*!

I put down my phone with a sigh. *These are just normal life things*, I tell myself. The kind of things I'd have to deal with no matter where I'd live or what I was doing. Homesteading wouldn't change that. In fact, if anything, it would probably add to my to-do list significantly.

It's just my to-do list would look different. Really different.

By the time Josh comes back with the kids, my equilibrium is mostly restored. The library books are by the door, ready to be returned, and I've added gluten-free cupcakes to my shopping list on the fridge and called the vet to schedule Max's appointment. I feel on top of things for the moment, at least.

And so I'm full of enthusiasm and cheer when everyone comes in, brandishing seeds as well as a raft of gardening equipment, several tomato plants, and a huge bag of compost. Josh is already lugging the tiller outside, a man clearly on a mission.

Inexplicably, William has lugged the bag of compost all the way inside, and it has split and is now trailing rich dark earth over my kitchen floor. Rose has already opened her packet of sunflower seeds and spilled them everywhere and is now near tears, and Bethany is asking me where her SAT prep book is, because she's wasted the whole morning. Meanwhile Jack is whacking the kitchen chairs with a brand-new shovel.

This is normal life, I realize, wherever we are and whatever we're doing, and it always will be. Moving to West Virginia is not going to change that.

"Okay, let's take all this stuff outside," I order. "Bethany, your book is probably up on your desk where you left it. Jack, put down that shovel *right now*. Rose, I'll help you gather the seeds." I stoop to collect a few. "William, that bag goes outside. And so does the shovel, Jack!" I take a deep breath. Smile. I feel surprisingly strong rather than my usual aggravated exasperation. "All right everyone," I say, "let's do this!"

Chapter Ten

D awn light is silvering the garden as I switch the coffeemaker on and Max stirs in his bed. It's five o'clock on a beautiful June morning, and I'm both exhausted and too wired to sleep. A lot has happened in the last few months... nothing has actually changed, and yet everything has.

First off, I learned just how much back-breaking work is involved in making a vegetable garden. I had hazy images of Josh enjoyably tilling up the rich, fertile New Jersey soil and then me scattering a few seeds in it while smiling and inexplicably wearing an apron, later looking on benevolently from the kitchen window where I am stirring my sourdough starter as the first tender green shoots push their way through the loamy soil.

I know, I *know*. If only real life came with a social media filter and a soundtrack. As it happened, Josh struggled even to get the tiller started. And then when he finally did, thanks to our neighbor Ben Wilson (we learned his name at long last), he struggled to operate it. The kids lost interest and drifted away, most to various screens; I flitted between offering Josh help and hiding in the kitchen. Josh flitted between good-humored self-deprecation and deep frustration. At one point, with extreme ineffectuality, he kicked the tiller and then winced as he hurt his foot, all witnessed by me from the kitchen.

"Maybe we're not meant to homestead," William observed as he joined me by the kitchen window. I didn't reply, but I was pretty much thinking the same thing. Something I'd noticed in my online perusal of various homesteading sites and blogs was that everyone always said how hard it was, and exclaimed how little they'd known when they'd started, but then they pretty much skipped over the rest to 'and then we built a bigger chicken coop and started our soap-making business.' Right now, that felt like an absurd and impossible leap. Yes, we'd been watching some videos and reading some online articles and thinking and feeling things, but when it came down to it? We were struggling to turn over a single square foot of suburban lawn.

Eventually, though, my dear husband persevered, got the thing going and then working, and he managed to till around a third of our backyard, churning up the lawn we had so carefully (well, sort of) maintained, keeping it trimmed and jewel-green for at least two months of the year. At the end of several hours' difficult work, the tilled-up patch looked... messy, all chunks of churned-up dirt and twisted roots, not the rich, black soil as fine as sand that I had been unrealistically envisioning.

In fact, our neighbors on the other side, whose names we *also* didn't know, were glancing at us suspiciously from their deck as we perused our new vegetable patch, because who wants neighbors with a yard that looks like a landfill site?

"We're making a vegetable garden," I called over at one point, and their frowns deepened into scowls. Homesteading in suburbia is not for the faint of heart.

Fortunately, things got a little better from there. Josh and I raked through the soil, plucking out the bits of twisted roots, and even though it was time-consuming work, and it made my fingernails black and my back ache, I found I liked it. Weirdly. The pile of discarded roots grew, and that was immensely satisfying. At one point, Rose, bored with her umpteen episodes of *Bluey*, came out and started helping, crowing in delight every time she liberated a root from the soil that was now starting to look the littlest bit loamier, the way I'd imagined it would. Jack, also bored, came out, and Josh gave him the challenge of finding more roots than he could. It was one our younger son took to with alacrity; he loved a little competition.

The sight of Jack and Rose rooting around in the dirt with us invariably had William and then Bethany drifting out, looking suspicious but interested, and by late afternoon we had everyone helping with the raking and the root pulling, turning our fledgling dream into something closer to a reality.

Only for half an hour or so, it's true, and we had to jolly them along before they all began to say how exhausted they were and one by one drifted back into the house. Still, it was a start.

To celebrate, we ordered pizza—we had to enjoy the conveniences of suburban life while we could—and watched the latest episodes of the Walkers' lives on YouTube as twilight settled on our barely-there garden.

The next morning, I was ready to plant seeds and Josh had to gently explain to me that there was a lot to do before then. Preparing the soil by raking in compost, first of all, and then, more importantly, building a fence.

"A fence?" I felt like he might as well have said we needed to build the Eiffel Tower. How on earth were we meant to build a fence? We didn't know how to do things like that.

"If we don't have a fence," Josh reminded me, "the deer will eat everything. You know how they always go for your perennials."

This was true. My gardening failures were not only due to my lack of skills but the deer that ate everything, relentlessly, which was often my excuse for not planting anything in the first place.

"How do we build a fence?" I asked.

"Good question."

And so Josh went back to the garden center and rented a fence post digger, as well as bought several dozen yards of chicken wire and fourteen fence posts. All of Sunday was spent building the fence; William came out and held the posts while Josh hammered, and even Jack helped with stringing the chicken wire. It wasn't the prettiest thing, it has to be said, and our neighbors were looking even more displeased by the jumbled mess of our backyard, but the fence was six feet high, and it ended up doing the trick. We kept the deer out.

Now it's the beginning of June, and our garden is full of fledgling plants—fragile tomatoes and orange-blossomed zucchini, spindly green beans and white-flowering peas, fern-like carrots and curly-topped lettuce, all pushing their bright green heads up through the rich, dark earth just as I once imagined.

Not to skip over to the easy part, as it can be tempting to do, because everything was as hard as all the blogs and videos warned, and we had a *lot* of failures. When the tomato plants were barely an inch high they all withered and died from an unexpected frost, and I ended up cheating and buying six-inch plants from the garden center, a place we'd barely set foot in but now knew us by name. I planted an entire row of peas that never came up. It was like the lost colony of Jamestown, vegetable style. I planted some raspberry bushes against the fence only to learn they wouldn't fruit for at least three years. Most damagingly, I once mixed up the fertilizer and pesticide and killed half our cucumbers before I realized my error.

And yet, despite all that, something about the garden got into my blood. The rhythm of it—planting, watering, weeding—ran over into the rest of our lives in a way I could have never expected and yet discovered I deeply enjoyed. And now here I am, waking up at an ungodly hour on purpose, rather than because Rose had a bad dream, or Max threw up after getting into the trash.

At dawn, the kitchen feels transformed. Everything is quiet, save for the twitter of birds from outside, and the comfortable grumble of the coffee maker, filling the room with its mouthwatering aroma. I stand by the kitchen window and watch a squirrel scamper up a tree, a deer appears at the edge of the woods, sniffing the morning air and, I imagine, looking longingly towards our garden full of young green plants. Fortunately, Josh's fence holds fast.

Over the last few months, Josh and I have taken three online courses—starting a garden, canning 101, and elements of an amateur homestead. Admittedly, a lot of the information has gone straight over our heads. The teachers have a friendly, folksy approach that I like but they generally assume a lot more base knowledge than either of us possess—yet. Because over the last two months, our knowledge, while still very patchy, has increased. And that's been a very empowering thing.

Growing and canning vegetables no longer feels like some kind of ethereal mystery. I know how much square footage you need per chicken for a coop and run. I've learned about companion planting, and how marigolds and tomatoes do well together, and how mint repels cabbage moths and zinnias attract ladybugs. So many things I never knew, that I never thought I would find interesting, and yet now I do.

What's been even better, though, has been the children's interest and involvement. Admittedly, *also* somewhat patchy, but growing. Rose has a corner of the garden for her sunflowers, now nearly a foot high. Jack likes to hack at the weeds, and William considers himself something of an expert in fence building and maintaining and has suggested several other areas of the lawn he could enclose in chicken wire, something I don't think would thrill our neighbors, but I encourage his new hobby all the same.

Bethany, sadly, is the only one who hasn't gotten fully on board, or, if I'm honest, on board at all, after that first fun day when we were all out there, making it happen. She has a part-time internship at a local pharmaceutical company doing boring admin work as well as a job at the checkout of our local ShopRite, and the endless hours of drudgery, as well as the fact she's going into her high-pressured senior year, have clearly taken their toll. She's become snappy and short-tempered with all of us, getting up early to get in a few hours of studying before she heads to her internship, and home late after the graveyard shift at the ShopRite.

It's no way for a seventeen-year-old to live, but whenever I've encouraged her to take a break, she gets cross with me. We're meant to be looking at colleges together in August and she's frantic about which ones we should visit, whether she should ask for a preliminary interview, how she can hype up her applications. When she comes home after work and sees us all on the patio, lolling about and enjoying the summer evening, she inwardly—and sometimes outwardly—fumes before stomping off to be by herself. Josh says to let her be, but I worry. Anytime I've tried to cajole her to come out with us, though, it's backfired, and she's doubled down on being too busy to be with her family.

To Bethany, I fear, the garden is no more than our mid-life crisis, a stupid hobby that we've created to amuse ourselves, and she is definitely *not* a part of it, which saddens me. I want to tell her that it feels like more than that, that somehow planting seeds has, sappily or not, planted something in me. I feel changed in a way I didn't expect to, but I know if I tried to share that with Bethany she'd just scoff and roll her eyes.

But I'm trying not to think about all that as I pour myself my first cup of coffee and curl up in the big armchair, Max on my feet, to enjoy the best part of the morning. This summer, the days feel slower, longer, with less frantic rushes to the local pool, hurling damp towels and sun lotion into a bag that has a lining of crushed goldfish crackers which cling to everything. There are fewer harried trips to Target, wilting in the humid heat, less plucking screens from sweaty hands or desperate scrolling on the computer for last-minute signups to summer camps the kids don't want to go to.

I'm not even sure why this is, because it's not as if we're all mucking around in the garden eight hours a day. The garden hasn't taken up *all* our time, not even close, but somehow it's *changed* us. I come in from the morning watering to find William and Jack doing a *puzzle*. Rose has developed a sudden interest in Hama beads and makes endless creations that I happily iron. Josh comes home from work and heads straight outside to survey his little kingdom, pluck a few weeds, and then plan another project.

Unfortunately—or fortunately, depending on my mood—there aren't too many more projects we can do in suburban New Jersey. I was right, our plot is too small to keep chickens. Until our vegetables ripen to the point of harvest, canning or preserving is merely theoretical. Josh cleaned out the garage—a long overdue task—and has started building a stockpile of tools we definitely don't need in our current life. He kept it secret, until one evening when I was putting out the recycling and stumbled upon a chainsaw.

"Why do we need a chainsaw," I asked him, "when we have exactly three trees in our backyard?"

He ducked his head, abashed but also a little bit defiant. "It was on sale."

"And we need it because...?" I didn't sound annoyed, though, but rather amused. He wasn't the only one buying things we didn't need. I had invested in way more Mason jars than any person has any right *or* need to own, and I'd bought things for the garden I hadn't yet used because I didn't even know what they were for. When the kind lady at the garden center told me I needed a seed mat, I gamely agreed and then promptly put it in our little potting shed, never to be used. She also recommended a self-composting bin that we can put all our vegetable peelings and grass cuttings in; so far, they have not turned into the promised rich black earth but remain a motley mix of eggshells and potato peels, but I'm still hopeful.

It felt as if Josh and I were both playacting at being pioneers in a way that was fun but also a little silly, and yet at the same time deeply satisfying. Satisfying enough that we didn't need to do anything more? That remained, as ever, the big question that we had not yet answered. It was only the beginning of the summer, after all. We weren't meant to reevaluate until August.

Now, tucked up in my armchair as I savor my first sip of coffee, I reach for my laptop with a slightly furtive excitement. Over the last few weeks, I've crossed a mental Rubicon and started looking online, secretly and somewhat obsessively, at property websites. I've saved my search, although I do vary it on occasion—at least five acres, anywhere in West Virginia or western parts of Virginia—goodness knows why I've fixated on that area, maybe only because Josh has—with a minimum of three bedrooms and a price limit of eight hundred thousand, which is about the price of our current home, according to Zillow.

There are a *lot* of houses out there, most of them ones I'd frankly rather not own, but occasionally I stumble on a gem that fills me with a sudden yearning for that picture window overlooking a pristine stand of pines, the wide front porch filled with flowerpots and rocking chairs, the neatly tended vegetable garden with a compost bin that works *and* a rain barrel, a cat perched contentedly on top.

I have not yet told Josh that I'm looking at houses, but I have a feeling he knows. I also have a feeling he's doing it, too. We might even be looking at the very same houses, favoriting them while looking over our shoulder to see if anyone has noticed what we're doing.

Even so, I can't help but suspect that this is still all part of the same, pie-in-the-sky dream—and that's what it will remain. Nothing more than a dream. The garden has been fun, and I'm glad we took the opportunity to slow down and savor it, but I still don't believe in my heart of hearts or even in the most logical part of my brain that we're going to move and actually *homestead*.

But, I tell myself, Josh's ideas always have a kernel of good sense in them, and I'm glad he got us all on this kick. For now, I can leave it at that.

I click on a house that was added less than twenty-four hours ago, and my heart skips a beat because, at first glance, it seems to have it all—the wide front porch, the picture window, the vegetable garden, the *life*. Then I see the price tag—just over a million dollars. Way out of even our most ambitious budget, not that we've actually set one.

But I look at that house and I love what it promises. In a house like that, I could slow down. I could can vegetables and knit sweaters and not lose my temper when Jack annoys Rose, or worry when William mopes, or feel anxious on Bethany's behalf. I could be the mom, the *person*, I want to be.

I'm still staring at my dream house when I hear the panicked shout from upstairs. I raise my gaze from the photo of the enormous master bedroom—complete with stone fireplace—as I realize it's *Josh* shouting. And he's crying out for someone to call 911.

Chapter Eleven

There are times in one's life that will forever be marked as 'before' and 'after', and this is one of them. That peaceful, sunny summer's morning is forever before. What the after is remains to be seen.

I am sitting in the hospital, staring at the sleeping form of my oldest child, feeling both empty and spent, as well as deeply, painfully terrified. All the simple pleasures and easy joys of our summer's garden have vanished like the morning mist I watched rise from my tomato plants. When Josh was asking someone to call 911, I had no idea who or what it was for. I don't think I thought at all, just fumbled for my phone and punched in the numbers. When the dispatcher answered, I stammered something incoherent, still not knowing what was wrong, until Josh came downstairs with Bethany in his arms, wrapped in a towel, dripping wet and unconscious.

The next few hours, thankfully, were a blur. The ambulance came; I went in it with Bethany, who still hadn't come to, her face pale and waxen, while Josh drove to the hospital in his car. We'd woken William, pale-faced and terrified, to man the home front until we knew what was going on.

What we learned was this: Bethany had collapsed from a combination of exhaustion, stress, and an overdose of caffeine pills. What her collapse had revealed was that she was seriously underweight and had been, judging by the score marks on her forearms, cutting herself for some time. Josh was so distressed when he saw those marks; he'd assumed they were from her eczema, and the doctor said some of them were, but the ones that weren't were still heartbreaking to see.

I felt both shocked and devastated, as well as horribly, heartwrenchingly guilty for not noticing that my daughter was self-destructing in front of my eyes. I'd been so consumed with living slowly and sustainably, eking some kind of meaning out of my mundane life, that I hadn't realized Bethany was drowning in her own anxiety and ambition.

That first day, I came home from the hospital while Josh took the night shift and went right to my beloved garden. I'd pulled up five tomato plants before William stopped me.

"Mom, *Mom.*" He ran into the garden, grabbing me by my shoulders to keep me from destroying another plant. "What are you *doing?*"

My face was wet with tears, and yet I felt more furious than anything else. Furious and heartbroken. "This garden almost cost your sister's life," I choked out. "I *hate* it."

"Mom, it didn't," William protested. He looked shaken, but his eyes were full of compassion. He took one of the plants I'd thrown aside and did his best to put it back in its hole, gently mounding the dirt around its wilted, ruined leaves. "You can't blame the garden."

I could, I thought, because it felt better than blaming myself. I sank right onto the dirt, my head in my hands.

"I should have seen something was wrong," I whispered. I *ached* with regret—every muscle, every bone. All our pioneering plans felt not just silly, but selfish. How could I have been more concerned for my precious pea shoots than my own daughter? How could I have dismissed her tension and snappiness, the glaringly obvious signs of unhappiness and exhaustion, so I could focus on feeling more present in my own little life?

I was angry as well as ashamed, and I never wanted to step foot in this garden again. But William was right, I decided dully. I shouldn't wreck it simply for my own sake. I would have to learn to live with my guilt. Somehow.

"I'm sorry, William," I said quietly as I wiped the grimy tears from my face. "I know it's not the garden's fault."

"And it's not yours, either," William replied with an impressive amount of emotional astuteness for a nearly fifteen-year-old boy. "Bethany's going to get better, Mom." It wasn't quite a question, but almost, and his face still looked pale and anxious. "I mean, she's not like, *sick*, is she?"

"No, she's not sick." Not in the way William meant, anyway. She was being kept in overnight as a precaution, but technically there was nothing wrong with her that a good night's sleep and a few square meals wouldn't solve. Nothing wrong with her physically, at least. As for mentally?

That's what I'm wondering now, on Bethany's second day in the hospital, as I gaze down at her face, peaceful in sleep. Why was she *cutting* herself, of all the horrible things? I'd talk to her about all the classic teenaged girl issues—self-harming, eating disorders, body image. Bethany had assured me, with what I now realize was too airy an attitude, that none of those was a problem for her. But meanwhile, secretly, she was hurting herself in a way I can't bear to imagine. The thought swamps me with both confusion and despair.

Yesterday we had to call her supervisor at the pharmaceutical company as well as at ShopRite to tell them she wouldn't be coming in for the foreseeable future, something that will probably infuriate her when we tell her, because knowing my daughter, she'll want to get right back on that horse and start to gallop away, even if it might be the worst thing for her. But that feels like a long way away, when yesterday Bethany had slept for sixteen hours straight, only waking to stare out the window without saying a word.

Where do we go from here?

Her eyes flutter open, and she stares at me groggily for a few seconds before she croaks, "Mom?"

I tuck a strand of honey-brown hair behind her ear, aching with love and sadness. "Yes, sweetheart?"

"How long have I been asleep?"

"A few hours. They decided to keep you in for one more night, just to be sure."

She frowns. "Sure of what?"

I decide not to tell her right now that the doctor in charge of her care wants her to see a psychologist before being discharged. "Sure you're okay," I reply lightly. "We've been worried, Bethany." I temper my words with an affectionate smile.

Her frown deepens as her gaze flits away. "I'm fine."

"You didn't seem so fine yesterday," I remind her as gently as I can.

"I was just overtired. I felt dizzy in the shower, and then I fainted. End of story."

"That's not quite the end of the story, though, is it?" I run a light fingertip along her forearm, where I can still see the signs of her cutting. They upset me more than anything else, as such vivid evidence of my daughter's unhappiness. How could I not have known, or at least suspected?

Bethany jerks her arm away and then relaxes it as a gusty sigh escapes her from the depths of her being. "It was just a stress reliever, Mom. Everyone does it."

Some stress reliever, I think with a shudder. "That doesn't make it a good thing to do," I tell Bethany quietly. "We're worried about you, sweetheart, and we want to help."

"What's the point, anyway," she mutters and closes her eyes.

I don't know what to say to that. I don't even know what to feel. Stewing in my own sense of guilt won't help my daughter, but I'm not sure what will. I want to have some magic words, a failsafe plan that will see us through, but I'm not sure there is any. We just need to get through this moment, and then the next, and the next, and the next. Right now, it feels endless.

"I don't want to go back to the internship," Bethany says with her eyes still closed. "Or the job at ShopRite. I hated them both."

"Okay," I say after a moment. Josh and I have never been pro-quitting, always advising our kids to stick out the unsavory if they can, but right now I am willing for Bethany to quit whatever she wants. "You don't have to go back. We can sort it out."

She turns her head away, her eyes still closed. "I'm not sure I want to go back for senior year, either," she whispers, and I lurch upright. Okay, I am not *that* much pro-quitting.

"Senior year is two months away, Beth," I remind her gently. "We don't need to think about that for a long time."

She keeps her eyes closed and doesn't reply.

The next few days pass in a different kind of drudgery. Two days after her collapse, Bethany comes home, quiet and frail, and spends hours in the armchair where I once enjoyed my morning coffee, simply staring into space, listless and silent. Everyone tiptoes around her, as uncertain and upset as if she has a terminal illness. None of us seem to know what the right way to be is.

She met with the psychologist in the hospital, and we've taken away all the razor blades in the house, locked them in the fireproof metal box with the passports and a safe deposit key. It felt over the top, almost ridiculous, and yet the fact that it wasn't, that the psychologist had advised us to do that very thing, was intensely, immensely sobering.

Bethany, we discovered, had been cutting herself for several months, probably since her second round of taking the SAT. She'd wanted to get a perfect score and was eighty points short, which is still utterly remarkable, but not enough for our driven daughter. I'd try to jolly her out of her glumness when she'd discovered her results; Josh had told her that her score was still in the top one percent of all SAT scores, and William had confirmed it with a quick internet search, telling her she was actually in the top *one-tenth* of a percent. Bethany had summoned a smile but not much more, and I had let it be enough.

Why had I let it be enough? Why had I let Bethany's endless ambition exasperate rather than alarm me?

The questions keep hammering through my head, but I have no answers. I was oblivious, so wrapped up in this whole *homesteading thing*, that I missed what was under my very nose. I vow to do better, whatever that means for our future.

I neglect my garden for a few days, because part of me still despises it, as irrational as that is, but then, one morning when everyone is still asleep, I find myself venturing out into the misty dawn and kneeling in the soft, dew-damp earth to weed a row of carrots. With each weed I take out, separating it with careful, tender hands from the fledgling carrot plant, I feel something in me both break and heal. I don't realize I am crying until the tears drip from the end of my nose onto my hand, but in a way they're good, or at least necessary, tears.

I keep weeding, trying to find both solace and strength in every liberated plant, every inch of cleared earth, but my heart is so heavy, and I feel a searing loss inside that a few minutes of *touching grass* won't help. The sun rises in the sky and starts to burn off the morning mist. It can't be much past six, and I don't think anyone else is up yet, and as much as I want this moment to matter and to heal, the despair inside me feels too deep. Then I hear footsteps, soft on the still-damp grass.

"Hey." Josh's voice is soft.

"Hey," I say back, in something of a croak.

"You okay?"

I shrug as I sit back on my heels. "Getting there, I guess."

He is silent for a moment, and then he hands me a mug of fresh coffee. I mumble my thanks as I cradle the mug between my hands.

"This didn't happen because we took our hands off the wheel," Josh finally says, his voice low. "You know how determined Bethany has been. We couldn't have stopped her, Abs, no matter what."

I'm not sure I believe that, as much as I might want to, and so I don't reply, simply taking a sip of my coffee. Josh sighs.

"Maybe this is a wakeup call," he says eventually.

"It's certainly been a wakeup call to me," I reply and my voice catches as more tears sting my eyes. It's only been four days since Bethany collapsed, and it all still feels so very raw. She still seems so very broken. I glance around at all my precious plants, and a despairing revulsion twists inside me. How could I have been so *blind*?

"What I mean is," Josh says carefully, "this is the wakeup call that shows us this life isn't working. For any of us."

I let out a sound that is half sob, half snort. "Really, Josh? *That's* your takeaway?"

"Okay," he replies evenly, "what's yours?"

I shake my head and take a sip of my coffee. I feel so empty inside, and yet at the same time swamped with misery. I look around the garden again. The tender pea shoots are ready to be carefully tied to their hoops. The first lettuces, bright green and frilly, will be ready to harvest in a week or two. The tomatoes have just formed on their vines, tiny and hard and green. There's so much promise here, and yet so much pain.

"My takeaway," I tell Josh in a hard voice, "is that we indulged ourselves in spinning our *Little House on the Prairie* fantasy and missed our daughter's cries for help. That I thought your dreams were harmless and even fun, sometimes exasperating yes, but never *dangerous*."

"*Abby*." He jerks back, startled and hurt by the venom in my tone. I'm surprised by it, too. I've blamed the garden, I've blamed myself, but can I really blame Josh, too? How can that possibly be fair?

Briefly, I close my eyes. "I'm sorry," I say. "I'm not saying this is your fault. Of course I'm not. But…" A long, low breath escapes me. "The dream ends here, Josh. Enough with the hours spent watching homesteading videos or spinning some life we're never actually going to have. We need to focus on what is real and happening *now*. Here, in our suburban house in New Jersey, with kids who need us *now*, not in some misty future in a mythical log cabin." I open my eyes and stare at him levelly, so he can see how utterly serious I am.

"There's another way to look at this," he insists quietly, and I already know the argument he's going to make, how homesteading is the *answer*, not the problem, and how our children, Bethany included, will thrive in such a different environment, away from both the pressures and drudgery of suburban life, able to work and learn and grow *together*.

"No," I cut him off before he can begin. "There's not. I'm done with all that, Josh. I'm done with dreaming about the alternatives. We have to focus on what's happening with our children *now*, in the real world, the world we inhabit. The whole homesteading thing?" I shake my head, a resolute back and forth. "It ends here. Now." The words thud through me, and for a second I want to take them back, but I don't. I stay silent and stare at my husband, letting him know just how much I mean it.

Josh stares back at me for a long moment. He looks unbearably sad, but also disappointed and even hurt. I've hurt him, I know, but still I say silent, and he doesn't offer any more arguments. He just nods slowly and walks back into the house.

I remain in the garden, my knees pressed into the dark earth, the world waking up to a beautiful summer's day. I'm not sure who feels more disappointed right now—my husband, or me.

Chapter Twelve

We limp through the next few weeks, all of us unsure how to be. Josh immerses himself in work, even though in the past he's always taken more time off in summer, to be with the kids. William plays a lot of chess online, hunched in front of the family computer while Rose becomes clingy, and I enroll Jack in a soccer camp he doesn't want to go to simply for him to have something to do. In our backyard the garden flourishes with weeds, so soon enough they blot out the plants I once nurtured so devotedly.

Occasionally I go out there and halfheartedly weed a row or retie a pea shoot or tomato plant, because it feels criminal to let all that effort go to waste, but my heart's not in it and that's obvious to everyone. I've always felt the mother sets the tone of a home, whether she wants that responsibility or not, and right now our tone is bleak.

Bethany hasn't gone back to her internship or her job at ShopRite; we called them both to explain, but I wondered if I should have made her do *something*. Instead, she spends hours curled up in the armchair in the family room, either staring into space or reading. She's gone back to her favorite childhood books, the ultimate comfort reads. There are far worse ways to self-soothe, but when I consider how switched on my smart daughter has been, there is something a little heartbreaking about her reading *A Little Princess* for hours on end.

She also goes to the psychologist recommended by her specialist once a week, although I have no idea what is said in those sessions or whether it's helpful. We've fallen back into the relentless groove we were in before Josh ever mentioned homesteading, and the truth is, there's not much that is comforting about it, even if it feels familiar. All the old issues rear their tiresome, irritable heads. Rose bursts into tears and wants people to do things for her. Even three hours of soccer every morning doesn't tire out Jack; he comes home restless and bored, annoying his siblings or demanding hours on the iPad, which I, exhausted and defeated before I've even begun, often end up giving him. William morosely plays chess online; when I suggest he attend one of the open sessions at the Princeton library, he flatly refuses. At the local club, he always plays with his friend Sanjeet, who is in India for the summer, visiting relatives. Without him, William seems more adrift than ever. And Bethany... Bethany is a shadow of her former self, and we all notice.

Life, which had once felt as if it were opening up into sun-filled possibility, starts to feel very small.

At the end of July, we head to the Jersey shore for our annual summer vacation—a week in the same semi-dilapidated beachfront condo we rent every year with my dad. Normally I enjoy the change of scene, the ease of having the beach right on our doorstep, the joy of watching my children run into the waves, but this year even these pleasures grate.

The boardwalk is loud and noisy, with teenagers playing music until well past midnight, even though it's against regulations. A smell of fried food from the various burger joints along the boardwalk lingers in the air, even in my *hair*. When I step through our sliding glass doors for the first time onto the beach, I nearly cut my foot on an old beer can. I had determined last summer that this year would be the one when Rose finally learns to swim, but she refuses to go past her ankles without floaties, sobbing piteously that she doesn't want to drown.

Jack is annoyed that we aren't willing to rent jet skis, even though he's too young to go on one, and on the first bright morning he declares that sandcastles and swimming—the two great pleasures of yesteryear—are totally boring. William, with his pale, freckled skin, stays inside or huddles under the sunshade, reading mangas and seeming as morose as ever. Bethany barely leaves her bedroom. Josh, who has always been the one to jolly everyone along, doesn't seem all that interested in being our ringleader. He halfheartedly asks Jack to go tubing with him, and he splashes in the water with Rose, but he seems as flat as the rest of us, and I can't really blame him. As a family vacation, it feels like a failure.

My dad, one of the most easygoing and affable people on the planet, takes it all in his stride. "Kids have their ups and downs," he tells me early one evening as we are walking along the beach by ourselves, the sun just starting to sink over the placid waves, giving them a rose-gold sheen. "Some of the downs are deeper and scarier than others. The important thing as a parent is you've got to weather both." He pauses, casting his gaze to the sky and quotes, "'To encounter triumph and disaster and treat those impostors just the same'."

"Rudyard Kipling," I reply, trying to summon a smile. *If* is my father's favorite poem, and I know it by heart simply by how much he quotes it. "It's different when it's not *your* triumph or disaster,"

I say quietly, "but your children's."

My dad nods sagely. "They're far harder to bear, it's true."

"If I knew what to do," I continue, confiding in my father in a way I haven't been able, or maybe willing, to with Josh. "I'd do it. I just want to *know*. Do I cheer Bethany on, try to get her back into the saddle, or do I let her be, because she needs some time to heal?" I shake my head. "I really have no idea which is the right thing to do. And the same with William. Should I drag him to a chess club, kicking and screaming, just to get him out of the house? It feels like he's retreating more and more into himself. I don't think he's made any friends in high school, and I know how hard that must be for him." My voice catches as I consider my eldest son, so smart and funny and shy. "I hate that for him," I tell my dad, a throb of emotion in my voice. "He's such a great kid, he deserves the kind of best friend who always has your back."

"I know," my dad replies softly. He reaches for my hand and gently squeezes my fingers. "Honey, I know. Watching your kids hurt is the hardest thing in the world."

"Was it this hard watching me hurt? Or Ryan?" Ryan is my older brother; he lives in New York City, works as a stockbroker, and cycles through high-powered girlfriends. We don't see him nearly as much as we should.

"It's always hard. Remember when you were in high school, and you lost out on that place at the Rutgers' summer science program? You worked so hard on that, coming up with your own proposal for an invention. Some steam-powered thing? You didn't want any help, were determined to prove everything by yourself. And then you didn't get in and you felt like your life was over." A wry smile tugs at his mouth, his faded blue eyes full of affection. "At least you acted as if it was."

I let out a soft huff of laughter. "Do you know, I'd completely forgotten about that?"

"Which might be a comfort to you now," my father tells me gently, "when you consider Bethany's situation. In time, she may very well forget too."

I breathe out, a gust of resignation. "This feels different, Dad. Have you seen her arms? They're covered in scars. The doctor said they'll heal in time, but she'd cut herself so many times. *Cut* herself." I still struggle to believe my little girl would do something so deliberately harmful. "For months, and I didn't even know."

"This is not your fault, Abby." Now my father sounds stern, or as stern as he can, because in reality my mom was the disciplinarian in our family. Pragmatic and cheerful, she was never afraid to tell Ryan and me like it was, or give us the punishment we deserved, while my dad would shoot us secretive, commiserating smiles and slip us treats when she wasn't looking. She died four years ago, from breast cancer, and I still miss her terribly.

"I know it's not my fault," I tell my dad. "Not exactly, anyway, but we got so wrapped up in all this homesteading stuff. I feel like we let ourselves get distracted by a stupid dream."

Over the last few months, I'd told my dad a little bit about Josh's homesteading fancies; he likes to check in by video call once a week and it was hard to not let some of it slip, considering how it had started consuming our lives, but I tried to make light of it all—the videos, the courses, the wild ideas. The kids told him about the garden, and as a keen patio gardener himself at his condo in Bucks County he was approving, but I never let on how seriously I'd been considering the whole thing. Still, judging by the thoughtful look on his face now, I think he might have guessed.

"Maybe it wasn't the dream distracting you," my dad says. "Maybe it's life distracting you from the dream."

"Oh, not you too," I retort before I can think to moderate my reply.

My father, as affably unfazed as ever, merely raises his eyebrows. "Touched a nerve?" he asks lightly.

"Josh and I have had a... disagreement about the whole thing," I confess with reluctance. Nearly a month on from that moment in the garden, and the whole homesteading idea is still a tense no-go area, which is so unlike us, and in particular, unlike Josh. Josh, like my dad, doesn't bear grudges. He shakes things off the way a dog shakes off rainwater and lopes onto the next thing, grin and goodness both restored. I'm the one who silently stews, who has to work hard to let something go, who needs Josh's cheerfulness to keep me from plummeting. Not having it now has been hard for not just me, or our marriage, but our family. Everything has felt depressing.

"He wants to give the homesteading idea a proper chance," my dad surmises with his usual smiling shrewdness. "And you, my dear, do not."

"I did," I tell him, "For a little while. Something about it seemed so... *freeing*. Breaking away from all the silly little things we've let chain us and grind us down. Choosing to live simply, to slow down, to prioritize our family..." I sigh, shaking my head. "Now all that sounds like a bunch of truisms."

"There's a reason they're called *tru*isms," my dad quips and I manage a tired laugh.

"*Dad*."

"Well, maybe I'm just being selfish," my dad says after a moment, a smile in his voice. "I like the thought of you homesteading somewhere because then I could come visit."

Something I hadn't actually thought of; one of my arguments against Josh's idea had been leaving family behind. But knowing my dad, he'd much rather spend time with us in rural West Virginia than suburban New Jersey.

"Have you not thought that Bethany's troubles might be a cry for help?" my dad asks quietly.

"I *know* they were a cry for help—"

"I mean, a cry for help. To say it's okay not to go to an Ivy League, or get straight A's, or be as accomplished as everyone else. She might feel like she needs permission."

"Okay." I absorb that slowly, accepting the idea might have some merit. "But, Dad, that doesn't mean we *move*."

"It doesn't mean you *don't* move," my dad counters. "You're viewing your life in Princeton as an ideal rather than a reality. Just because it's the option currently on the table doesn't mean it's the best one."

I stop right there in the sand to stare hard at my father. "Did Josh pay you to say all this?" I demand. I'm only half-joking.

"No," my dad laughs. "Josh hasn't said a word, Scout's honor. I've just been seeing how miserable you are, my darling, and it's made me wonder why. For someone who gave up what you say is a stupid dream, you don't seem all that relieved about it."

I am silent then, because my dad, in his gently astute way, has hit the nail right on its unfortunate head. I'm *not* relieved. I'm not even close to relieved. Instead, I am miserable, and disappointed, depressed and angry. It's not a great way to be. It's not a great way for my kids to see me being.

But as I stand there on the beach, oblivious to the spectacular sunset of crimson and gold unfolding in front of my eyes, I still don't relent. Maybe I'm just being stubborn, but after everything that happened to Bethany, uprooting her to some fantasy pioneer life is not the answer.

It can't be.

"I hear what you're saying," I tell my dad as we keep walking. "And I'll think about it."

My father nods, a small, sad smile tugging at his lips, because I think he knows as well as I do that I just told a lie.

By the end of the week, we've all rallied, at least a little bit. Rose learns to swim, thanks to William's patient instruction, and Josh and Jack went tubing for a whole afternoon, to both of their excitement. Bethany ventures out, as cautious as a snail, and reads her book—*Jane of Lantern Hill*—while sunning herself on a beach towel. I start to remember what normal feels like.

My dad, as kind and patient as ever, picks up the slack—he makes pancakes one morning, and plays endless games of Crazy Eights with Rose, and watches William's online chess game with alert attentiveness even though he barely knows how to play. I am very grateful to him in helping us recover our equilibrium, even if it feels as if we're just grazing it with our fingertips.

As we troop back into our house, tired and sunburned with a mountain of laundry to do and Max, liberated from his week-long kennel stay, joyfully bounding around us all, I almost feel like my old self. *This is my life*, I remind myself, *and it's not so bad*.

Then Jack lets out a shriek, the kind that has my shoulders tensing toward my ears. "*Mom*! Look!"

"What..." I fear a burst pipe, or rats in the garbage we forgot to take out, or something green and furry in the fridge. All are perfectly possible.

"The garden!" He points out of the kitchen to the garden, which looks like even more of a riot of weeds than it was before we left. A week in July, with several days' rainfall, has turned it wild and rampant.

"Yes," I say wearily, trying to force a pragmatic smile, "we've let it go a little."

"Not that," Jack says impatiently. "I mean, the tomatoes! And the peas! Look!"

I crane my neck to peer a bit more closely through the window, and then I see it. The glint of a red tomato between all the wild weeds. Fat pea pods practically falling off their stalks. While we've been away, feeling sorry for ourselves—at least I have—our garden has grown. It's flourished, despite the weeds and neglect.

Jack yanks open the sliding glass door with a screech and sprints out to the garden. Rose runs after him, while William cautiously follows, and Bethany stands by the open door, watching.

"Look!" Jack yells and holds up the thick, twisted stalk of a zucchini plant. "Can I pick one? Can I? Can I?"

"Um..." I am baffled and bemused by his infectious excitement as well as the garden's growth. "I suppose so."

"There are *tons*," Jack crows gleefully and Bethany surprises me by saying,

"Let me get a basket."

Slowly I follow my children out to the garden. Josh is still hauling suitcases from the car, and I almost call to him, but I know he won't hear me. And in truth, I don't know how I feel about our garden growing while we were away, in *spite* of my own intransigence. I am sheepish and surprised and strangely moved. It's a lot to process. I stand by the garden gate while my children get to work. Bethany holds the basket while Jack twists tomatoes off the vine like he's been born to it, and Rose collects fat peapods in the hem of her t-shirt. William is inspecting everything else in the garden, calling out a commentary.

"The green beans are doing well—I'd say they could be harvested. There are lots coming, too. And the onions are practically bursting out of the ground! I think the carrots have suffered a little, but maybe they just take longer..."

I lean against the fence post, my heart full, as I watch them all work together to collect the harvest I hadn't expected. As thankful as I am, my gratitude is tinged with a sorrow that I still can't dispel. But maybe that's just the way life is—you never escape the shadows, you just learn to find the light.

"What's going on here?" Josh calls as he walks through the sliding doors we left open in our exodus outside.

"Dad, look!" From Rose, jumping up and down. "My sunflowers!"

"There are *so* many tomatoes, Dad," Bethany says. While her tone is still somewhat muted, it's the first time I've heard anything close to enthusiasm in ages. I meet Josh's gaze, expecting a slightly smug told-you-so look in his eyes, but instead his expression is tender, which just about undoes me.

"This looks great, guys," he says. "Thanks to everyone's hard work, Mom's especially. We all did it."

Chapter Thirteen

The next few weeks are taken up by our newfound family operation of reaping the unexpected bounty of our garden. How do you actually *can* tomatoes? I took an online canning class, but it felt different in practice, and I was glad for the endless videos on YouTube as well as the mechanical canner Josh bought so we didn't have to spend endless hours heating the jars in the oven.

I also appreciated the very logical point William made that we didn't actually *eat* canned tomatoes all that much, and he didn't think they sounded all that appetizing, but we did eat a lot of spaghetti sauce, so maybe we should make that instead. Bethany roused herself to make three different kinds of tomato sauce and then had Josh taste test them all before we settled on the one we wanted to preserve in jars.

Then there was all the other bounty from the garden—zucchini as big as baseball bats (I learned later you're not meant to let them grow that big); peas bursting from their pods; onions bulging up from the ground; carrots that were small and sweet and tender-crisp. Jack took over the job of digging for potatoes like he was mining for gold—searching for them in the dirt, crowing in triumph when he found them, and getting completely filthy in the process.

William was our math guy, figuring out how many jars we needed, how many tomatoes per jar, and keeping track of everything we managed to preserve—and it was a lot. The glass jars with their jewel-like contents were stacking up in the pantry and it made me feel both proud and grateful.

It still didn't change my mind, though. I could tell Josh was hoping it would, and part of me wanted to relent, at least a little, until I remembered what he was asking and just how big a leap it would be—for all of us. Bethany was going into her senior year. Jack was getting occupational therapy for his ADHD. Rose was attached at the hip to her best friend, and when Sanjeet came back, William would be too, at least at chess club. We weren't going anywhere.

And yet even in August, tiny things chipped away at my certainties. William read an article in *The Economist* about food security and set off a conversation at dinner one night about how many people would be completely stuck if the food supply chain was disrupted.

"Do you know only four countries in the entire world create enough food for their populations?" he asked us seriously. "The US, along with Canada, Australia, and Ukraine. That's *it*. If food supply chains get disrupted, it could be seriously bad news for some countries."

"It could," Josh agreed, while I stayed silent. I'd always insisted I didn't care about an abstract concept like food security, but it was hard to see it as abstract when our pantry was full of jars of our own produce, and we'd already seen food supply chains disrupted during Covid.

Another night, in the middle of August, that in-between time when the weather was still sticky and hot, but a few leaves were already tinged with scarlet, Rose clambers onto my lap. She's grown several inches this summer, and she had her seventh birthday at the end of July. She's learned to swim and we're hoping—with some serious parental coaxing—to get the training wheels off her bike by the end of the summer.

"Why don't we watch the Walker videos anymore?" she asks unexpectedly. It's been several months since we've all watched one together. "I liked them."

"I liked them too," I reply dutifully. "But maybe we watched so many we got tired of them." As Josh is in the room, I try not to sound too pointed.

"But I want to know if Murphy had kittens," Rose continues, a note of insistence entering her sweet little voice. "And whether Amy sold her eggs to that grocery store." Nine-year-old Amy Walker had been hoping to start her own egg business. We stopped watching when Murphy was pregnant with her second litter of kittens. It's strange, to think how invested we'd become in a family we didn't even know and never would. The dangers of social media, I suppose.

"Yeah, I want to know if Tom built that second barn," William says suddenly, his tone rising in the same way Rose's had. "He designed it himself and everything."

"And what about the homesteading convention they were going to go to?" Bethany asks. "Weren't they going to be, like, the speakers or something?"

I had not known there were such things as homesteading conventions until I watched the Walkers. "I don't know," I say as I slide Rose off my lap and head to the kitchen to finish loading the dishwasher.

A silence follows this pronouncement, until Jack fills in the obvious. "Well, we could watch it again, couldn't we?" he asks, his tone wobbling with uncertainty as he senses the tension I've introduced into the room. "And find out?"

"Yes, let's watch again," Rose cries. "On your bed, like before!"

I realize I do not want to watch the Walkers with us all piled up on our bed the way we did before —before Bethany, before my eyes were yanked open to how costly it is to lose yourself in a dream. I don't say anything and after a few seconds Josh fills in quietly,

"Maybe another time, guys."

Which makes me feel so much worse, and so reluctantly I relent. "I guess we could watch one video," I say, the words drawn from me slowly. I don't meet Josh's eye as the kids let up a ragged cheer and Jack and Rose race for the stairs, followed by William and Bethany. Everybody seems game.

Josh stops me at the bottom of the stairs; by the sounds of it, the kids are already fighting for pole position on our bed. "We don't have to do this," he says, laying a hand on my arm.

I give a twitchy sort of shrug. "It's fine," I tell him. "It's no big deal."

"Abby—"

I walk past him up the stairs, pretending I haven't heard him, only to feel horribly guilty for doing so, and I turn around. "I'm sorry," I tell him. "I know I'm being a downer. It's like I've forgotten how *not* to be."

Josh joins me on the stairs, wrapping his arms around me. I lean into him, grateful for his strength. It's been a while, I realize, since we've hugged. Too long. As I'm on the stair above him, we are almost eye level, and he pulls back a little to gaze at me seriously.

"Abby, I took what you said on board," he tells me, like a promise. "I'm not pushing the homesteading thing anymore, I promise."

The Homesteading Thing, the words I have used to dismiss the idea, in my mind. It hurts somehow, to hear Josh talking about it the same way.

"I know you're not," I tell him, an ache in my voice. "I'm... I'm sorry."

He frowns. "What are you sorry for?"

"Destroying your dream. I still feel the way I do, but I could have been kinder about it all."

"Well." He gives me a lopsided smile as he releases my shoulders. "Emotions have been running pretty high."

"Mom, Dad!" William yells. "There are *fifteen* new episodes! And Tom built the barn!"

He sounds so exultant that I can't help but smile. "I guess we need to go catch up with the Walkers."

"I guess so." Josh drops a kiss on my head. "I love you," he tells me. "Whatever we do, wherever we do or don't go. That won't change, Abby."

My throat is thick, and I have to swallow before I answer. "I love you, too," I tell him. "And that won't change, either."

He smiles at me once more before we head upstairs to join our kids, all piled on our bed, laptop at the ready.

"Mom, Dad," Jack says excitedly as he pats the empty space next to him. "Come *on*!"

I snuggle in next to Jack, Rose on my lap, as Josh sits on the other side, his arm around William. Bethany perches on the edge, not quite committing, but not leaving, either.

We press play on the first video we'd missed, uploaded six weeks ago. Within minutes we're all immersed in the Walkers' lives, but this time it doesn't seem quite as magical to me. It doesn't seem *bad*, either, just more real.

Did Sarah Walker always have such dark circles under her eyes? Admittedly, as a mom to six kids and a full-time homesteader, she has every right to look more than a little tired, but somehow I missed the streaks of gray in her hair, the way her shoulders occasionally slump. And Tom, the second oldest boy who wants to build his own barn, was he always so truculent? He and Jay get into an argument about safely using the circular saw that has me wanting to ground him for a week, not that I'd even know what that looked like, homesteading-style. When Murphy has her eight kittens, Amy is elated, but Sarah looks like she's not thrilled about taking care of yet more animals, although she summons a weary smile to her lips. They are all cuddling kittens by the fire as the familiar soundtrack—a rejigging of an old John Denver song—starts up, their classic closing music, as the video slowly fades to black.

Add a soundtrack and a soft-focus filter, and *anything* looks appealing, I suppose, and yet somehow the arguments and the tiredness and the low-level chaos that is always bubbling away under the surface doesn't make the Walkers' life look less appealing, but maybe even more so, because it *isn't* a dream. It's gritty and real, with all the small-time hassles of my life now, and yet so much more.

It's *possible.*

It's a lot to think about as the kids tumble off the bed and I head back downstairs to finish loading the dishwasher. Josh comes down to let Max out, and neither of us speak as we move around the kitchen. I don't know what I'd say if I did, because my thoughts are so jumbled. Watching the Walkers again stirred up all sorts of things inside of me that I was very happy, or at least willing, to leave untouched and unthought of. Now I take comfort in the mundane routines of tidying up the kitchen, wiping counters, cleaning up the mess as my mind empties out. Josh lets Max back in and then heads to the corner of the living room that we turned into his study to do some work.

I stand alone in the kitchen, glancing around the familiar space like it's a place I don't recognize, simultaneously trying to figure out how I feel and not wanting to know. After a few minutes, Rose skips down the stairs and comes over to me, wrapping her arms around my waist. I ruffle her soft, strawberry-blond hair as she whispers against my stomach,

"Can we move to a house like the Walkers and homestead?"

It's like she was reading my mind, and for a second I am jolted. "You really want to do that?" I ask.

"I want a cat," she replies, and I remember my foolish promise, that if we moved, we could get a cat.

"Maybe we'll get a cat right here in New Jersey," I tell her rashly, and she beams up at me, joyfully incredulous.

"*Really?*"

"Maybe," I reply, and now I sound cautious. How many foolhardy promises am I going to make just to keep from thinking too hard about what we're *not* going to do?

Chapter Fourteen

T he rest of August slips by surprisingly fast; we harvest the rest of the garden, so the pantry is pleasingly full. I almost get sick of having so much produce—did we really need that many potatoes? And I have no idea why I planted radishes, because no one likes them. Does anyone? But overall, the garden was a success, and by the time school is starting up, life feels normal again, or almost.

Bethany is still quiet, but she hasn't mentioned not going back to school. Josh has lost a little of his bounce, but he's cheerful with the kids—playing chess with—and losing to—William , throwing a baseball around with Jack, tucking Rose in at night. He spends several hours one evening helping Bethany craft her essay for the common application; she's the one to stop first, saying her brain hurts and who needs to define courage, anyway? We let it go, because we're still in baby steps territory—we ended up not going on that college trip because she didn't want to—and I'm not sure I can define courage, either, at least not in a pithy and clever way like she'll need to do in an essay.

Life falls into norms that aren't hassle-free, but they aren't depressingly mundane, either. The school run, the grocery shop, the dog walk, the carpool, the twenty-minute wait for band practice to get out, the suddenly sprung homework project that's due *tomorrow* and requires a glue gun, craft paper *and* poster paints... these things don't bring me down the way they used to. Life feels very manageable, which is no bad thing.

The restlessness I felt in the spring, when we were watching all the homesteading videos and Josh was dreaming about acreage has left me at long last, and I'm back in the mode of slogging through life while trying to be a little more aware of the joys. *Lesson learned,* I think, *and we didn't even have to move.* Which was what I wanted all along, so it's all good, except...

Things start to happen. Little things, the kind of things that might annoy or anger me, but they wouldn't give me pause. They *shouldn't* give me pause, because Josh and I made our minds up—well, I made them up for us—and we're not moving. The *Homesteading Thing* is officially over.

And lots of things are going well. Bethany is happy enough to go to school, even if she's less than enthused about her college applications, and doesn't seem interested in visiting any nearby, despite my hesitant suggestions. Princeton, Rutgers, Penn are all less than an hour away; we could do it in an afternoon, I tell her, but she just puts me off, says she has too much homework and she knows what they're like anyway.

William is enjoying chess club, and he and Sanjeet compete together at a tournament in Cherry Hill. William is triumphant because he beats the former seven-year-old—now eight—with the personal coach. Jack's therapy appointments are going well, and we tried a new medication that keeps him on more of an even keel. He even was Star of the Week for being helpful in class, which is a first. Rose and Chloe are still happily best friends, and Rose has learned to tie her shoes, ride a bike, and lost her front tooth, without freaking out about the blood. Too much, anyway. All successes, in my mind, except...

Bethany comes home one wet Wednesday in early October and announces she's quitting band practice.

"What?" I am standing by the sink, a dripping sponge in hand. Max, sprawled by the kitchen table, lifts his head from his paws to gaze worriedly at Bethany, alarmed by her tone. "Why?"

She flings her flute case onto the floor where it lands with an alarming clunk, considering how much that tube of metal cost. "I just don't want to do it anymore."

"Bethany..."

"The only reason I did it," she fires at me, "is so it would look good on my college applications. And I don't think I want to go to college anymore."

I drop the sponge into the sink. "Okay," I say after a moment, trying not to sound as freaked out as I feel. Josh and I have always told the kids that we want to support them in whatever they choose to do in life, and we absolutely do, but... not go to college? All right, maybe some of Princeton's competitive spirit has seeped into me.

"What's made you think that?" I ask, mentally congratulating myself for sounding merely curious.

"Oh, I don't know, Mom," she retorts, rolling her eyes, "you wanted me to go to an Ivy even more than I did."

Okay, maybe I didn't pull off that inquisitive tone as much as I thought I did, but that's not fair. "Bethany, I want you to go to the college that's right for you, whatever that is." *That* I know I mean.

"But," she counters, her eyes gleaming with the triumph of winning an argument against a parent, "you still want me to go to college."

I sigh, deciding to concede the point. "I suppose I always thought that was something you would do." I wait for her to reply, but she just shrugs. "If you didn't go to college," I ask, "what would you do?"

"I don't know." Another shrug. "Maybe start my own business."

"Start your own business?" I can't quite keep the disbelieving surprise out of my voice. She has never once mentioned starting her own business.

"Ruth did it," she flings at me, and it takes me a second to realize who she meant.

Ruth Walker, who at fourteen years old bred her own chickens and started an egg business, supplying neighbors and even a local farmer's market. At least, according to YouTube.

"So what kind of business would you start?" I ask her, genuinely curious now. How much has Bethany been thinking about this? Maybe she inherited more of Josh's adventurous spirit than I'd ever realized.

"I don't know. Something."

Hmm. "Bethany, are you sure this isn't you just feeling a little frazzled about the whole application process? I know it can be challenging—"

"*Please* don't patronize me." Her eyes flash. "I've had a lot of time to think about this. It isn't some random idea I just thought up because I've watched too many YouTube videos, okay?"

Considering that is pretty much exactly what I thought, I decide to keep silent.

"I just want *out*," Bethany says quietly, and the throb in her voice tells me she means it. "From everything."

"Okay," I say after a moment. "Well, we have Columbus Day

weekend coming up. We could go away for a few days—"

"That's not what I mean." She still sounds quiet, and that scares me. I know she isn't self-harming anymore, and her counseling sessions seem to help, but she's still painfully thin and if I'm honest, she's been willing to go to school, but she hasn't exactly been happy about it.

"Okay," I say again. "So maybe you, Dad, and I need to sit down and think about next steps."

"And then you'll just try to convince me to go to college?" she says, and now she sounds weary and even sad.

"No, we won't do that," I say slowly, "but we need to have some kind of plan, Bethany, don't you think? Don't you want that, too?"

For a second her face crumples, and then it smooths out and she sighs. "I guess so," she replies, and I feel relieved. We'll all talk, and Josh will jolly her along, and she'll apply to college—any college—after all. And if she doesn't, at least we'll figure something else out. A gap year, building houses in Alabama or Peru or somewhere that gives her a fresh perspective. It'll be okay.

But while we're figuring out a good time for that all important chat, other things happen. Jack comes home, despondent because his fifth-grade teacher has gone off on maternity leave and the new teacher, an old battleaxe named Mrs. Jamison, 'doesn't believe in ADHD.'

"What do you mean, she doesn't believe in it?" I ask him when he shows me the note in his backpack—a warning that if he continues to misbehave he'll be given a detention. "Did she actually say that?"

"She said it was just an excuse for little boys to be naughty."

The woman sounds like a throwback from the 1950s. "Dad and I will talk to her," I tell Jack, but if I mean to reassure him, I fail utterly.

"You can't do that!" he exclaims in panic. "Everyone will find out and then I'll be such a *loser*."

"Jack, lots of parents talk to their children's teacher." Especially in Princeton, practically the birthplace of helicopter parenting. "It's not a bad thing."

"If you do, I'll never forgive you," he tells me dramatically. "Never ever ever."

It's another thing to bring up with Josh, but he's so busy now, working more than he ever has before, and I haven't stopped long enough to wonder why—never mind ask him about it.

The next domino to fall is William. One day he doesn't get up for school and when I come upstairs I find him still in bed with the duvet pulled up over his head.

"William... are you sick?"

"Yes," he says, his voice muffled.

"What? Stomach, or...?" Gently I pull down the duvet. William stares at me, looking not very sick but very much miserable. Downstairs I hear the door slam shut as Bethany heads out to the school bus. She turned seventeen in July, but she hasn't been motivated to get her driver's license, much to my chagrin. New Jersey is the only state where you have to be seventeen to drive, and I was really counting on Bethany being able to do the school run.

"William...?" I prompt gently. "What's going on?"

"I just don't want to go to school."

"Why not?"

"I don't like it." He thrusts his lower lip out. "I never did."

Something I've always suspected but hoped would get better with time. I sit on the edge of the bed. "Why don't you like it?"

"I just don't."

I have a feeling we're going to go around in circles, and so I decide to leave it for now. "I think maybe you need a rest day," I tell him. "I'll let you stay home today, but only if we can talk about this and figure out a way forward, whatever that looks like. Okay?"

A wave of relief passes over his face at the thought of not having to go to school. "Okay," he promises. "We can talk."

I have a feeling our conversation will be akin to pulling teeth, and I'm meant to be working today, but I can make time for a chat. I hope. Josh is at the office today, otherwise I'd ask him to have a man-to-man with William, but I am uncomfortably aware that the number of things Josh and I need to talk about is piling up.

What's going to be next?

Chapter Fifteen

J osh and I finally get our chance to talk on Columbus Day weekend. We didn't end up going anywhere, but we get the Monday off and we head to a local farm to pick pumpkins. It almost feels like a normal, happy day, except for all the problems pressing down on me. Bethany still not wanting to go to college. Jack bringing home warnings from his teacher at least twice a week; he's already had one detention. I still haven't called the school, simply because he's so panicked about it, but something clearly needs to be done.

As for William... we had a conversation the day he stayed home, sitting in the family room with cups of tea, but it didn't really lead anywhere. I asked him why he didn't like school, and when he gave me the usual non-answer, burying his nose in his mug, I asked, in as gentle and roundabout way as I could, was it because he'd had trouble finding friends.

William had looked up at me in disgust. "So you think I'm a total geek with no friends? *Thanks.*"

"William, I didn't say that—"

"You basically did."

"Well, who *are* your friends?" I asked in something close to exasperation. "You never talk about them."

He shrugged. "Just because I don't talk about them doesn't mean

I don't have them."

Which was a triple negative and took me a second to untangle. "All right, well, tell me who they are," I said in what I hoped was a reasonable tone. "Give me some names."

William glared at me for a second before muttering, "Daniel." He put down his mug and folded his arms. "And Rasheed."

"Okay..." I had never heard these names before, but of course I wouldn't have, because William never talked about anyone.

"You think I'm lying, don't you," he accused. "You think I made them up. How pathetic do you think I am, Mom?"

"I don't think you're pathetic," I cried. "I think you're a wonderful, smart, funny boy and if people don't appreciate that—"

"Just stop," William groaned, grabbing a throw pillow and pressing it to his face. "You are making me feel, like, a *thousand* times worse."

So I stopped, and that's where we left it. William went to school the next day, looking morose, and I felt miserably guilty *and* worried, which is a toxic combination for any mother.

But now, as we're all picking out our pumpkins, and it's one of those gorgeous autumn days that feels as warm as summer but with the lovely crispness of fall, my heart lifts with hope and I tell myself we can weather these storms. Nothing is too terrible, after all, and we'll find a way forward for all of our children.

Josh and I are heading to the Tiger's Tale tonight for our biannual drink—the last time we went was nearly nine months ago, when he first mentioned homesteading—so we can talk it all through. Josh has always been great at talking me down from my panic and fearmongering, the worst-case scenarios I spin out in my mind where Bethany lives in our basement for the rest of our lives, Jack becomes a juvenile delinquent, and William is in therapy for his high school trauma. At least Rose seems to be doing okay, but maybe it's just a matter of time. Maybe it is for everyone. No one's life is smooth sailing all the way through, after all.

"Bethany is still saying she doesn't want to go to college," I state without preamble as soon as we've ordered our drinks. "I'm worried about her. It's already the middle of October—"

"She doesn't have to go to college," Josh replies with a shrug. "If she doesn't want to. In any case, a year out could be a good thing for her. I've talked to her about volunteering at the lavender farm out toward Belle Mead."

For a second, I can only gape. "Wait—what? You've talked to her? And about the *lavender farm*?" I don't think we've ever been there, although we drive by it often. It looks like a pretty enough place, although I always wonder how on earth they make a living.

"She's interested in doing something more tied to the land," he tells me. "And her time at the pharmaceutical company made her realize she doesn't want to go into that kind of field. She was thinking about focusing on creating products with more natural elements."

I'm not even sure what that means. What products? What natural elements? Besides, Bethany has, for her entire middle and high school career, been focused on a career in STEM. And now she wants to volunteer at the hippy lavender farm?

"Okay," I say after a pause. "I... I didn't realize you'd had this conversation."

"Well, I think she felt you were pretty focused on the college track."

"Only because this is a pretty major life decision to suddenly do a complete one-eighty on," I reply, stung. "I know she's had a hard few months, but that doesn't mean she has to throw it all in—"

Josh leans forward, his eyes alight but his expression grim. "She's not throwing it all in, Abby," he says. "Throwing it all in would be going to college when it's really something you don't want to do."

"Josh, she's *seventeen*. Are you sure she even knows what she wants?"

"You know our Bethany. She's always known her own mind."

Which I have to admit is true. She was the most stubborn toddler alive, insisting on doing everything herself, even when she couldn't possibly manage it. It's admirable in retrospect, utterly aggravating in the moment.

"Okay," I finally relent. "So she lives at home and volunteers at the lavender farm?"

"And maybe works part-time too. She's thought about it, Abby. I know it isn't what we expected or maybe even hoped, but if it's what she wants..."

"Okay." It takes me a moment to absorb and accept this, because while I'm not actually disappointed, I'm still worried. It's such an about face that I can't help but wonder if she'll regret it a few months in. But maybe that's part of growing up—learning who you are and what you want to do.

The waitress comes with our order—a glass of white wine for me and a beer for Josh—and for a few moments we are simply silent, sipping our drinks. I'm glad Josh had that conversation with Bethany, really glad, but it's thrown me. I'm usually the one who has the heart-to-hearts with our kids. Josh is more of the lighthearted jolly-along type.

"And William," I say eventually. "He's not enjoying high school. I asked him if it was because of—of his social situation, but he said it wasn't."

"I know." Josh nods. "I talked to him about that."

"You talked to William, too?" This comes out in a surprised yelp.

Josh raises his eyebrows. "Am I not meant to talk to my own children?"

"No, of course not. I'm glad. It's just... you've been so busy at work, and... and I thought I was the one who usually had these conversations." I smile a bit shamefacedly, because when I say it out loud it sounds a little self-aggrandizing, like I'm the only one who can manage our kids' emotional lives.

"Well, I made the time," Josh replies evenly. "I could tell something was wrong."

"And so did William tell you what was going on with school?"

Josh shrugs and takes a sip of his beer. "Just that he finds the classes boring and there are a lot of try-hards—his words—who are so competitive they won't even share their notes. So you're right, it is a little bit of a social situation thing, because he hasn't really found his tribe, but it's more than that. He just doesn't like it."

Once again it takes me a moment to absorb and accept. "So have you come up with a solution?" I ask finally.

"We've talked about a few things," Josh replies after a moment. "Online school, where he can choose the level of his courses, or maybe a private school, if we can afford it, but he's not sure about that, because he thinks the whole atmosphere will probably be worse."

"Okay." Once again, I find I am reeling. How did all these conversations happen without me knowing? And why did I think I had to be in charge of everything? "And Jack?" I ask, managing to let out a little laugh. "Have you sorted him out, too?"

Josh gives me a wry smile. "No, I haven't cracked that nut," he says. "Jack is adamant we don't talk to his teacher and so until his other teacher comes back from maternity leave, I think we're in for a bumpy ride."

"If she comes back," I reply glumly.

"Next year he'll be in middle school," Josh reminds me. "Maybe that will be okay."

Or maybe it will be worse. I sigh and take a sip of wine. "And Rose? Have you had any conversations with her?"

"Well, I've read her *The Story of Ping* approximately two hundred and twenty-seven times," Josh replies, "and we've discussed in depth what will happen when her other front tooth falls out, but other than that, no. I don't think she's having a major crisis, but maybe wait a few years."

"Or months," I only semi-joke. I pause, my wine glass half-raised to my lips. "And you, Josh?" I ask quietly. "How are you doing?"

For the first time, Josh's gaze slides away from mine. "I'm okay," he says quietly, and with a lurch I realize he sounds anything but. I knew he'd lost a little of his usual bounce, but I didn't think *he* was in crisis. I depend on him to be the steady one; yes, he gets carried away with his dreams, but he's always cheerful and good-humored about it.

"Do you mean that?" I ask hesitantly.

Josh's gaze swings back to me. For a second, I don't think he's going to respond. Then he lets out a gusty sigh and says, "What do you want me to say, Abby? I'm okay. *Just* okay. I don't like my job, I never have, if I'm honest, but I'm all right at it and I know it pays the bills and keeps a roof over our heads. I don't like suburban life or the Princeton area, with its hyper competitiveness and helicopter parenting, but I've learned to live with it all." He pauses, looking as if he might stop before plowing ahead resolutely, "Sometimes I feel like I'm staring at the rest of my life doing exactly the same thing until I'm as good as dead and it fills me with either despair or panic, but then the feeling goes away, and I do my best to move on." He leans forward, a glint of something in his eyes—not anger, no, but desperation. "So yes, I'm *okay*."

I stare at him in wordless horror, speechless with shock at the depth of his emotion, the darkness of his feeling. How did I not guess any of that? And how on earth am I meant to respond?

Chapter Sixteen

J osh holds my gaze, a fire now lighting his hazel eyes; maybe he is angry as well as desperate. And why shouldn't he be, when I clearly haven't been paying attention? At least not as much as I should have. I gape gormlessly at him, struggling to think of what to say, or even what to feel. I had no idea my lighthearted dreamer of a husband had this depth of dark feeling in him, and I really don't know what to do with this new and unwelcome realization. I have always depended on Josh to be the light, laughing one. He brings me out of my panicky moods; he keeps me from getting too anxious about all the details. But maybe I've been selfish, depending on him in that way when he so clearly hasn't been able to depend on me.

"Josh..." I begin helplessly. I honestly don't know what to say. I feel winded with shock, but also heavy with sorrow—and yet more guilt. I've missed so much in my family's life, and all the while I thought I was the one keeping all the balls in the air.

Josh finally breaks my gaze. "Maybe I shouldn't have said all that," he says heavily, which is different than saying he didn't mean it. Very different.

"No... I'm glad you did," I tell him, although I'm not entirely sure I mean that. "We need to be honest with each other." Even if it leaves me reeling.

He sighs. "Even if it doesn't change anything? What's the point, then?"

I jerk back, even more shocked by just how dispirited he sounds. This is not my Josh. I don't *like* this Josh; I feel sad and scared for him in a way that upends all my certainties about our life together, our *marriage*. "What do you mean, it won't change anything?" My voice quivers. "Josh..." Again I stop.

Josh's face settles into implacable lines. "Face it, Abby, you've set yourself against the whole homesteading idea—"

"Are you honestly telling me homesteading is the only thing that will make you happy?" I retort before I can think to temper my reply. But, *come on*. Lots of people live perfectly satisfactory lives without reenacting *Little House on the Prairie*. And while I got into it for a while, absolutely, I don't think I ever thought it was something we'd be doing full time, for the rest of our lives.

"We just keep going around in circles," Josh says with a sigh that is somewhere between weary and disgusted. "I want one thing, you want another. Who compromises? Who gives in?"

I stiffen. "We don't necessarily have to look at it like that—"

He levels me with a look. "Don't we?"

"Josh..." For the third time, I feel helpless. I'm used to Josh being cheerful, coaxing, or otherwise just willing to let it go. I've never seen this hard-faced obduracy from him before, and it both scares and unsettles me. What happened to my happy husband?

He sighs and picks up his beer. "I'm not sure what more there is to say. You've decided this isn't something you're willing to do, no matter that all the kids are on board with it—"

"All the kids?" I break in, trying to scoff but not quite managing it. "Really?"

Once again he gives me a disconcertingly level look. "Have you talked to them recently, Abby, about something that matters? Not just managing them, or making sure we all stay on track, but really seeking their hearts?"

I make some kind of noise, because *seeking their hearts* is not number one on my priority list. I don't parent according to Hallmark. "And you have?" I ask, managing not to sound *completely* incredulous.

"I have," Josh replies with a touch of proud defiance. "William hates his high school. He has friends, a few anyway, but the classes bore him, and he wants to do something different. Bethany has had it up to here with this whole pressured lifestyle. Jack longs for more action, something he can really sink his teeth into, and Rose—well..." He gives me a lopsided smile. "Rose wants a cat."

I let out a laugh, because that much is true. But as for the rest...? Have I really missed so much? Closed my eyes and ears and yes, my heart, to it?

Am I the only one resisting this?

"And you?" I ask quietly, because I know I need to know.

"And I want more out of this life," Josh states in a tone that is heartfelt without being over-the-top, with a thrum of sincerity that I know I can't doubt. "I want to spend serious time with my kids, teaching them things, learning together. I want to wake up in the morning and look forward to a day where I work with my hands and eat the food I helped to grow. I want to feel like I'm putting down roots, *actual* roots, rather than continually skating on the surface of life, only to flop into bed, exhausted and wondering what I've done with my day, my time, *myself*. And I know homesteading won't be easy," he adds, before I can interject, although I'm not sure I was about to.

"It's backbreaking work all day long, and utterly relentless and incredibly hard. But that's what I *want*, Abby." He leans forward, the desperate light in his eyes seeming to plead with me to understand. "I want to work by the sweat of my own brow. I want to feel like I created something, and it was *good*. I want to build a life I can pass onto my children if they choose to take it. But most of all, I want to do all that with *you*." He sits back, satisfied or maybe defeated, I'm not sure which.

A beat of silence passes, stretches between us. I know his heartfelt declaration needs a reply, but I don't know what it should be. "I don't know what to say," I finally admit as I gaze down at my barely touched wine. "This... this has thrown me." That is definitely an understatement. I was, I realize, skating by on the surface of life, just as Josh said, assuming that everything was, if not fine, then at least good enough.

But is good enough actually my aspiration? And *is* it even good enough? The questions thud through me, and I know I'm not ready to think about their answers, even as they thud through me too.

No, it's not. Not nearly.

"I'm sorry," I burst out. "I didn't realize... I didn't realize this was about me, and how I've... failed." The thought that almost brings tears to my eyes. I shake my head, blinking rapidly so nothing spills. "Josh... what do you want me to do?"

"Abby, I don't want you to do anything," he says tiredly. "This isn't about me convincing you, or you *failing*. You haven't failed, Abby. We just want different things out of life right now. It happens."

Ouch. I blink to absorb that matter-of-fact statement, because it sounds awfully final. Josh could not possibly be saying...

"I know I tried to convince you, back in the beginning," he continues. "I was so excited, and I wanted you to be, too. But... I can't make you feel something you don't feel. I don't even want to try. So..." He lets out a long, weary breath. "Since we're married and we love each other, where does that leave us? Someone has either to change or to be willing to compromise. Or maybe both of us do. I don't know." He shakes his head, seeming so defeated that my heart aches, and yet I can't help but feel relieved that Josh isn't implying we've grown irrevocably far apart. I definitely do not want that.

So what do I want? The answer comes with surprising speed—I want my husband back. I want him happy, with that light in his eyes I love so much. But what does that mean for me?

I sit back, shaking my head in wonder as the realizations continue to course through me. I had no idea that this went so deep for Josh... and yet at the same time, I think I knew it did. At least, I suspected. I'm not, I realized, as shocked as I'm acting. On some level, I knew how important this whole *Homesteading Thing* was to Josh, and maybe even to the kids. So the question that remains is... what am I going to do about it?

"I'm sorry I've come across as so stubborn," I offer hesitantly. "After Bethany..."

"I know what happened to Bethany shook you up," Josh says quietly. "But Abby, surely you can see that Bethany didn't crash and burn because we were so involved in a *vegetable garden*. It was so much more for her than that."

When he says it like that, it seems glaringly obvious, and yet...

Did I just use Bethany's wobble to back away from something that scared me? And if so, then the question is, *why* did it scare me so much?

And what am I going to do about *that*?

There are way too many questions for me to figure out the answers to, at least over a glass of wine at the Tiger's Tale. My brain hurts along with my heart, because the truth is, I really, really don't like seeing my husband so unhappy.

"Okay." I force my resolute gaze back to Josh's weary one. "What would you like me to do, Josh? What steps would you like me to take? I'm not saying I'll definitely take them," I add quickly, because even now I need that caveat, "but I'm certainly willing to think about them. Seriously."

Josh stares at me for a long moment. "I don't want to drag you along, kicking and screaming," he says finally.

"I promise, I won't be kicking and screaming." Not much, anyway.

"Okay." He blows out a breath. "Then maybe... go to a homesteading convention? As a family?"

For a second, I gape. A *homesteading convention*? I'm picturing the *Little House on the Prairie* version of a *Star Trek* convention, with people milling around a stale-smelling convention hall wearing bonnets and aprons.

"Is there one?" I ask uncertainly. "I mean, you have one in mind...?"

"The Modern Homesteading convention in Virginia is in January," he tells me swiftly. "There will be workshops, speakers, events, vendors... it's just a chance to explore the world, Abby. Get some more information."

"Okay." I don't sound thrilled, because I don't *feel* thrilled, but one weekend is not that much of an ask. "Where would we stay?"

"The convention is at a fairground, and most people camp there, but if you'd rather, we could stay in a hotel nearby."

We have never been hardy campers, which begs the question of whether we could actually homestead, but I am not about to go down that route right now. "Camping in January might be a little intense for us," I tell my husband with a small smile. "Why don't we stay in a hotel, at least this time?"

Josh grins, and it's like the sunlight streaming from behind the clouds, brightening up the whole world. I didn't realize just how dispirited he's looked all these weeks until I see him like this—that old gleam in his eyes, the playful smile about his lips, that buzzy sense of energy that is infectious and that I *need*.

"Great," he says as he rubs his hands together. "I'll book the tickets. There's stuff for the kids, too. I think they'll really enjoy it."

"Right." I feel a flicker of my old enthusiasm, the excitement for this new life that I ruthlessly quenched when Bethany was rushed to the hospital. Maybe it won't take as much as I thought it would to get it back. A convention could be fun, and we'll have some family time, which is a plus. This could work. This could be good.

Chapter Seventeen

In mid-December, about a month after Josh's and my painful heart-to-heart, I go to my book club, having read a book summary online and grabbed a bottle of wine from the local liquor store on the way. Not the best way to treat pretty much the biggest social event in my calendar, but that's where I'm at right now. I haven't seen any of my book club friends since the last book club I went to, back in April. I missed June and the first one in fall, and we skipped the summer months in between, because everyone was so busy.

Such is life. Such is *this* life, anyway.

These are the kinds of thoughts I've been thinking as I've bustled and hustled through the last month—Thanksgiving with my dad; planning Christmas with Josh's parents; cards to send, presents to buy, parent-teacher conferences to attend, a virtual work event because my company is too cheap to pay for a party, plus all the rigamarole of regular life—vet appointments, dry cleaning to pick up, groceries to buy, a stomach bug that wreaked havoc on every single member of our family for an entire week. And so another month both dragged and flew by, as they always seem to do.

"Abby!" Kerry air-kisses both my cheeks as I step across the threshold. Her foyer is decorated with white Christmas lights and smells like an evergreen candle. "Hello, stranger! *Very* long time, no see," she exclaims as she steps back. "How *are* you?"

"All right," I say, summoning a smile. I hand her the mid-range bottle of wine I brought and she takes it, clucking that I shouldn't have. I see her lips purse as she glances at the label, and I have a feeling it will be regifted over Christmas. I'm not really offended; I'd probably do the same.

As I follow her into the kitchen, I am acutely aware that I never told her about Bethany's meltdown, and I know I'm not about to now, which begs the question of how strong our friendship really is or ever has been. "How are you?" I ask.

"Oh, we're great," Kerry enthuses. "*So* great. Isabel got an early admission offer to Dartmouth yesterday." She says this like they've won the lottery, which they basically have, collegiate-style, but also with the false, nonchalant modesty of someone who is trying not to come across like they're bragging when they so obviously are. And I do *not* feel envious, I tell myself sternly, before I realize with a jolt of surprise that it's true. I do not want Bethany to go to Dartmouth or any other Ivy League, not when I've seen what an intense academic environment does to my lovely daughter.

"Wow, that's so amazing," I tell my friend, and we do another round of air kisses to celebrate.

I kind of want to go home already, but I tell myself not to be such a grump. Kerry is my friend, and I'm happy for Isabel. Of course I am.

"*Abby*." Lindsay wafts in from the family room, wearing a lot of cream cashmere and looking effortlessly elegant, which means it probably took her an hour to get ready. Goodness, I've become cynical. I'm annoying myself with my petty thoughts, but it's like I've hopped on the train to snarkland and I don't know how to get off.

Ever since I agreed to go to the homesteading convention—now a little less than a month away—I am feeling weirdly panicky about my current life, both losing it and living it. It's like I can't win.

Josh is super excited, though, and we spent an evening last week going through all the workshops on offer, from churning butter—Lindsay's joke made reality—to successful sourdough, cheesemaking for beginners, permaculture design, the family milk cow, hog butchering and sheep shearing. There were less practical and more philosophical workshops as well—*How to Involve Your Children So They Love It*! And *Building Community like the Amish Do*.

I admit, some of those titles and descriptions gave me a flicker of curiosity, even of excitement. Some of it made me suppress a shudder of horror. Hog butchering? No thank you. But Josh was enlivened, and that I liked to see. A lot. And the kids were excited too, just as Josh had predicted they would be. William wants to attend a workshop on ways to prepare for an off-grid home, Jack one on outdoor survival skills, and Bethany is keen to go to the Herbs for Humans course. Rose loves the child-friendly options on offer—a playground made of hay bales, a craft tent with plenty of possibilities, and the opportunity to travel around in a golf cart.

All in all, it's looking like it would be an incredible if overwhelming weekend. We've already made our reservations at a Holiday Inn two miles from the fairground.

"Lindsay," I greet my friend, unconsciously parroting her overly warm tone. "*So* good to see you."

Lindsay cocks her head, as if sensing some sarcasm but not quite believing it, and I give myself a serious mental kick. *Get over yourself, Abby. These are your friends.*

"It's been a long time," she remarks as she takes a sip of her wine. "What have you been up to?"

"Oh…" I think of Bethany's hospital stay, the bounty of the vegetable garden, William's troubles with high school and Jack's difficult new teacher, and of course, the convention coming up. "This and that."

Lindsay's eyebrows rise. "You're not still off on that homesteading thing, are you?" *That Homesteading Thing*, just as I've always, somewhat derisively, called it. The words thud through me, and I swallow hard. "Well…" For a second I think of dismissing the idea, pretending homesteading really was just a silly and passing fad, but then I know I can't, and more importantly, I don't even want to. "Actually," I say, "we're going to a—a homesteading convention next month."

For a few agonizing seconds Lindsay and Kerry both just stare at me, completely nonplussed by the announcement. I might as well have just told them we were becoming Amish.

"I didn't even know such things existed," Lindsay murmurs, shaking her head.

"I know, right?" I try to laugh. "I didn't either, but to tell you the truth, it all seems pretty interesting. Compelling, even. I mean…" My voice is growing stronger as I feel my sense of conviction unexpectedly kick in. "Getting back to nature, eating healthily, spending more time with your children, teaching them to be resilient and self-reliant… honestly, what's not to love about that kind of lifestyle?"

"When you put it like that," Kerry admits with a funny little laugh, "it sounds different. Appealing, even." But she doesn't sound remotely convinced, and neither did I, back in the day.

Have I really changed? How did that happen, when I wasn't even trying? In fact, I was actively trying *not* to change. Somehow I did, anyway. A little, at least.

Fortunately, someone else arrives then, and my homesteading adventure is momentarily forgotten. For the rest of the evening, I sit on the sofa and listen to the impassioned chat about a book I haven't read and have no desire to as what I told my friends reverberates through me over and over again. *I meant it*, I realize with a kind of dawning wonder. *I really meant it.*

I am still thinking through that stupefying realization as I say goodbye at the end of a long and laborious evening, having promised Kerry we would 'really, really meet up soon', as we always say and never seem to do. I imagine us drifting even farther apart over the next few years, occasionally bumping into each other at Wegmans with expressions of surprised delight and making yet more meaningless promises.

As I let myself into the darkened house, I find Bethany at the kitchen table, her chin in her hands as she studies her laptop.

"Hey." I drop my keys into the bowl. "It's late."

She shrugs. "It's a Friday."

"True." I nod to her laptop. "What are you up to?"

Bethany tenses, and I am conscious of how *cautious* our interactions have been over the last few months, both of us afraid to give or take offense, I'm not sure which. Bethany seems to hear accusation in everything I say; I hear judgment in her tone. She gets offended; I back away. Rinse and repeat, endlessly.

"I'm just looking at some stuff," she replies, sounding guarded.

"Dad mentioned you were thinking of volunteering at the lavender farm next year." I haven't had a chance to talk to her about it, and it's been almost a month. Guilt upon guilt. Why didn't I make time for this conversation weeks ago? I know the answer, of course. Because life was so busy. Because it's easier just to keep going and add it to your mental to-do list than actually *talk*.

"Yeah." Bethany smiles shyly, still looking hesitant. "I emailed them, and they said I could come have a chat in January."

"That's great, Bethany."

My voice is warm, and she regards me skeptically. "Is it?"

I give her a frank look, wanting to be honest, and more importantly, wanting her to be honest. "Do you think so?"

"Yes, but..." She pauses. "I didn't think you would."

I pull out a chair and sit across from her at the kitchen table. The only light is from a side lamp, and the room is warm and cozy, the yard outside the sliding glass doors cloaked in wintry darkness. This feels like the right time for a chat. "Bethany," I tell my daughter, "I want you to do something that makes you happy."

A smile plays about her mouth. "Even if that was drug dealing?"

I let out a guffaw. "Well, there are limits."

Bethany's smile drops as she looks at me with an endearingly uncertain earnestness. "Seriously... I thought you'd mind. Me not going to college, I mean."

"If I seemed like I minded," I answer carefully, "it's because I thought *you'd* mind. I didn't want you to regret making a decision you made when you were going through something."

"I suppose that's fair," Bethany replies, which feels like a first. "And maybe I will regret it, but I can always go to college later. I just... *can't* now. I can't put myself through all the stress, feeling like I'm behind everyone, all the time." She closes her laptop, her forehead furrowed. "Everyone's getting their early decision acceptances or rejections now, and all I feel is relieved that I don't even have to *think* about it." She glances up at me, her expression clearing. "Honestly, Mom, this is the best thing for me right now. I mean that."

"I'm glad." I hesitate and then ask in as offhand a manner as I can manage, "And this homesteading thing? Dad said you might be pro that?"

She laughs, a pure sound. "Yeah, maybe. Kind of wild, huh? I mean, are we really going to live in a log cabin and keep chickens?"

I shake my head, smiling, feeling lighter than I have in a long while. "Honestly? Right now it feels like we might."

She frowns. "But you don't want to?"

"I've had my reservations," I admit. "It's such a major life choice. But..." I exhale slowly as I glance around the darkened kitchen. "I thought this life was working, that it was enough for all of us, but then Dad has made me wonder if maybe we are missing out on something. If maybe living differently could be good for our family." I pause and then admit, "Really good, even."

Bethany nods somberly, seeming to completely get—and agree—with my confession. "Yeah, you know, I've been feeling the same way. Like maybe it *could*."

We are both silent, absorbing our admissions. *Homesteading here we come*, I think wryly, and for the first time in a long while, it doesn't fill me with fear. The dread that has swirled in my stomach for so long is slowly but surely dissipating.

I realize that this is the longest and most positive conversation I've had with my daughter in over a year, and that knowledge both humbles me and fills me with hope. Change is possible. This life we're seeking, it can be found. We just need to know where—and how—to look for it.

Chapter Eighteen

The Westmont Fairground in a small town in the Shenandoah Valley is bustling with activity and sparkling with frost. There are tents everywhere, along with people—guys in lumberjack shirts and well-worn hiking boots, women in jeans but also long skirts and yes, there are a couple of bonnets visible amidst the milling crowds.

We arrived in Virginia last night to our hotel, and we've just stepped across the threshold of the Modern Homesteaders Annual Conference, underneath a striped banner that welcomed us to the 'Heart of America'. It doesn't feel politicized in this place, though, despite the plethora of American flags; everyone is too focused on living the good life. The air is filled with the smell of woodsmoke and roasting meat, and rings with different sounds—hammers on iron, the squawk of chickens, the laughter of children. It's overwhelming, but in a good way. I don't know where to look first.

"What should we do first?" my dad asks, as if he could read my mind. Yes, my dad decided to come along for the ride. I went out to visit him after Christmas, and over brunch in Bucks County he insisted that he wanted to join our adventure.

"What's not to like?" he asked me, like it was obvious there was nothing. "It sounds amazing."

"Would you really want to homestead?" I asked, laughing. "You could come live with us."

"Only if you wanted me to," my dad replied, sounding far more serious than I'd expected him. With a jolt, it hit me that my dad might be *lonely*. I didn't visit him nearly as much as I should have or wanted to.

But maybe that could change...

"There's an orientation for first-timers," Josh says. He sounds ebullient; he's been buzzing for weeks at the thought of coming here. "I think we should go to that, and then we can peel off to various workshops."

We head to the tent that's for first-timers; holding a convention outside in January is not for the faint of heart, and I'm glad we all bundled up, even though I'm still cold. Rose slips her hand into my hand and skips along as Jack bounds ahead, and William and Bethany drift together, my dad ambling nearby, taking in all the sights. We're all glad to be here; it feels like a big step, and *that* feels like a good thing.

"Hey, first-timers!" a man in a flannel plaid shirt and jeans greets us cheerfully. He has a bushy beard and flyaway gray hair tamed by a well-worn baseball cap. "Welcome to MHA and find yourselves a seat. There's coffee over there, if you want it, good and hot."

We murmur our own greetings as I move toward the coffee. I want something to warm me up as well as keep me occupied, because the truth is I feel nervous, like a sixth grader on the first day of middle school, all gawky shyness and painful hope. Josh is looking around like he's expecting to find his best friend, and my heart fills with love for him. Whatever comes from attending this thing, I'm so happy for him. He's got his mojo back for sure.

With steaming cups of what is indeed very good coffee in hand,

Josh and I head for some seats right at the front, thanks to my keen jellybean husband. I sit down with a rueful smile for my dad, who just grins back. He's clearly loving every moment of this. The kids file in behind us, filling up a half a row.

A few more people filter in, and they really seem like a cross section of humanity—some look uncertain like I'm sure we do, while others swagger and some laugh and joke with the guy at the door. I exchange a few smiles with a couple of the women—a young woman who can't be more than thirty with a baby in a sling and a toddler clinging to her hand; a woman in her mid-fifties with a bright red bob and a humorous look on her face, like she can't quite believe that she's here.

Or maybe I'm just projecting.

After smiling around at everyone who meets my eye—and there are quite a few people who do—I settle back into my seat to see who is going to lead our orientation. To my shock and amazement, I recognize the couple who come to the front of the makeshift stage, dressed warmly in fleeces and jeans and hiking boots, pretty much standard wear around here.

It's Sarah and Jay Walker.

"Mom!" William hisses, looking starstruck. "It's the *Walkers*!" Jack and Bethany are whispering about it, too, looking just as impressed to see the YouTubers we've been watching for months just ten feet away from us.

I nod my understanding, hardly able to believe it; they hadn't been listed on the conference speaker lineup, or any of the workshop presenters. Are they just here as normal people? They feel like rockstars.

"Hey, everyone," Sarah greets us, as Jay waves and offers a wry,

"Howdy."

A cheer goes up from the crowd, and I realize that in the home-steading world, the Walkers *are* rockstars. And, at the same time, they're just normal people... like us.

Sure enough, Sarah launches into an anecdote about the first convention they went to, right when they'd decided to make the move to Tennessee but hadn't yet made that leap of faith.

"There we were," she relates, her voice full of laughter, "still living in a three-bedroom townhouse in Georgetown, with a yard no big-ger than a postage stamp, *seriously*... and we were trying to remember how to pluck a chicken and milk a cow and can green beans... I mean, I hadn't done any of it yet. I just knew that I wanted to."

There is laughter, and sagely understanding nods, and a few mur-murs of agreement. Everyone here, I think, is in *something* of the same place we are. Sarah goes on to say how she learned, and how friendly and accepting everyone here is, and how willing and even eager they are to help "us newbies".

"Because six years on," she finishes, "we still feel like newbies, especially compared to the families who have been doing this for *generations*." She nods earnestly, accepting of our silent, seeming disbelief. "It's incredible, guys, it really is, to see people living as nature and God intended them to... and I mean that absolutely." She holds up a hand. "No judgment for the way other people might choose to live, but y'all are here, and you *chose* to be here, and that's a wonderful, wonderful thing."

My mind is still buzzing with all the information as she and Jay relay all the practical details about exits and bathrooms and places to get water. Rose is tugging on my hand, already eager to explore, and the other kids look just as expectant. We're all *ready* for this.

At the end of the orientation, the Walkers are mobbed, and so I decide not to say hello and head out into the fairground. I have a cheesemaking workshop to get to, after all.

The sun is shining and it's crisp and cold, the kind of day where you want to fill your lungs with fresh air even if it hurts a little bit. William is heading to the off-grid workshop, surprisingly content to go alone, and Bethany has decided to check out some herbal vendors. My dad has offered to take Jack to an axe-throwing tent, and Josh is heading to a class on building and maintaining your barns and sheds. Rose decides she wants to make some cheese with me.

We walk along, stopping often to peruse one vendor or another; there's an old-timer with a two-foot-long beard doing the most exquisite wood carving; at another stall a man is blowing glass, creating perfect bubbles of fragile translucence. Everyone here is busy doing—creating, working, helping, *being*. It's a good feeling, and it makes me want to be part of it. I squeeze Rose's hand as we hurry along. I don't want to be late to our workshop.

"This is fun, Mommy," Rose says as we head to the tent. I glance down at her, a little surprised, because we haven't yet checked out the hay bale playground or the children's craft tent. And yet... when was the last time it was just Rose and me together? So often she's been an add-on to the other kids, accompanying me on carpools and doctor appointments, simply because I couldn't leave her at home alone. I smile down at her as I squeeze her hand again.

"Yes," I agree. "This is fun."

We make our way to the mozzarella-making tent, which is set up with various portable stovetops equipped with large pots. The woman running the workshop is red-cheeked, with a long gray braid down her back and a wide smile, and she gestures for us to take up position in front of one of the stovetops, along with a couple in their late twenties who look as abashed and uncertain as I feel.

We make introductions—they live in Cleveland, Ohio and are trying to eke out a sustainable existence on a quarter of an acre in the suburbs.

"We'd love to buy a couple of acres somewhere, maybe in Georgia or Arkansas," the woman says wistfully, "but it's just not possible right now."

"And not for a long while," the man adds glumly, before rallying with a rueful smile.

I give them a commiserating smile back, but the truth is their admission humbles me. I've been debating—and resisting—such a move without even considering that for many people it's no more than an unobtainable dream and might always be.

Check your privilege, I remind myself, unironically for once. If we sold our house in Princeton, we could certainly buy some acreage in West Virginia, probably with some money leftover if we didn't splurge on the kind of properties I once was daydreaming about. But for a lot of people, like this young couple, it remains an unaffordable dream. Why did I never consider that before? Why was I so negative, right from the beginning, always coming from a place of skepticism and even scorn rather than genuine, openhearted inquiry?

I don't have time to delve any deeper into my psyche, because it's time to make mozzarella. The workshop leader, Barb, guides us through measuring out rennet and citric acid and dissolving them separately in water, and then stirring the milk until it reaches ninety degrees. Then we add the rennet and cover the mixture for five minutes; Rose is agog, eager to find out what has happened to the milk.

"So do you guys have a homestead?" Dave, the young man working with us, asks, and I admit, somewhat apologetically, that we don't, we're just investigating at this stage. It feels like a copout.

"But we're going to," Rose announces with chirpy confidence. "We're going to buy five acres in West Virginia *and* have a cow and a cat."

"Rose," I protest, bemused, but Dave is smiling.

"That sounds awesome," he tells Rose sincerely, and I kind of agree with him.

I touch her hair as I smile down at her. "Why five acres?" I ask.

"That's what Daddy says we need to be self… self… self-sustaining," Rose replies, smiling proudly, and it is a reminder that our youngest child is always listening.

Five minutes later, the milk and rennet mixture has set to the consistency of thick yogurt, which delights and disgusts Rose in just about equal measure.

"Ew, Mommy, you can *cut* it!" she exclaims as Barb instructs us to cut the curds into a grid and then heat them to one hundred and six degrees. Rose keeps an eye on the thermometer as I stir; Dave and his wife Jenna have their own pot of curds to deal with.

I watch, mesmerized as if by a miracle, as the curds separate from the whey. When Barb says as much, Rose chortles with delight.

"Just like Little Miss Muffet!" she tells me, and I have to laugh. We scoop the curds up and deposit them in a colander lined with cheesecloth—"*that's* why it's called cheesecloth, Mommy, see?"—and wait for them to drain.

Another five minutes later—we've chatted to Dave and Jenna about their dream property, with a log cabin, a large vegetable patch and space for chickens and a family milk cow—we are heating up the whey liquid and adding the curds, and soon enough it's time to don rubber gloves—Rose's are enormous on her little hands—and pull and stretch the curds like taffy. It's remarkably satisfying, to pull it long and fold it over, until the curds are shiny and firm and basically *look* like mozzarella, which really does feel miraculous. Then it's time to roll them into balls, which Rose loves, and dip them in ice water to set.

I can't believe it, but I've actually *made cheese*. I feel ridiculously proud as well as incredulous that we actually did it, that it's even possible to do, and when Barb lets us pack up the cheese we made in a plastic container to take with us, I am also excited to show my family just what we accomplished. So is Rose, crowing all the way back to our designated meeting place, about how she can't wait to show everybody and taste it herself.

"Me too, Rose," I tell her as I take her hand, and she skips along. I find I can't stop grinning. "Me, too."

Chapter Nineteen

The next twenty-four hours pass in a whirlwind. In a spirit of pragmatism, Josh and I agreed to do as many workshops as we could, so we hardly spend any time together over the course of the conference, and we collapse into bed on Saturday night too exhausted to do much but exchange sleepy information.

"Permaculture is definitely the way to go."

"A family milk cow provides up to eight gallons a *day*."

"Forty meat chickens should be enough for a year."

"I'm not sure it's worth keeping goats."

I can't quite believe these are the thoughts we are having, and yet they *are*. My mind is full of them. The kids, too, are buzzing with all they've learned. Bethany talks my ear off for half an hour over dinner about the healing properties of ashwagandha and William lectures Josh on how to divide up the five acres we don't yet have.

"Obviously, most of the land will have to be given over to the livestock," he says, like it's a no-brainer, while Josh nods seriously.

I'd wonder how we could have possibly got here, except I'm agreeing with him. We need at least an acre for our cow, and another half-acre for the chickens. That is, according to all the experienced homesteaders I've talked to, who are friendly and free with advice without sounding know-it-all or judgmental. I'm a complete and utter greenhorn, and yet nobody makes me feel like one.

Instead, everyone laughing shares their own mistakes, gently imparts their learned wisdom. I listen, rapt, as they show me this whole new world, a world I'd barely begun to glimpse back in Princeton.

By Sunday morning, I feel like it's been a wonderful weekend, even if my brain is packed full and my heart is overflowing. If Josh asked me right now if I wanted to homestead, it would be a heartfelt and unequivocal yes, but when we get back home and there are two loads of laundry to deal with, and homework to check on, doctor's appointments to schedule, and a job I've let go by the wayside, as well as the friends I'll need to text back, promising to meet up even if we never do... will I think so then?

I still have doubts. Even in my current state of ebullience, I wonder how this could possibly work and if real people do this, even though plenty of people who *do* are all around me.

My dad must sense that, because as we are eating breakfast in the hotel lobby—one of those all-you-can-eat buffets where there is not actually all that much you want to eat—he plops down next to me with a cup of coffee.

"It's been a good weekend, hasn't it," he remarks. "Full on, but good."

"It has," I agree. My dad has accompanied various children to their workshops, happy to slot in wherever he's helpful. I'm very grateful. All that's left is the concluding speaker later this morning and then we'll be heading home. The thought makes me feel a little tug of sadness.

"But you're not sure," my dad remarks, a statement of fact. "Still."

"Still?" I raise my eyebrows as I summon a laugh. "Dad, it's been one weekend."

"Abby," he replied, his voice gentling, "it's been almost a year. I know when Josh first mentioned this idea, because you told me yourself."

And that seems like a million years ago now. "That's true," I concede, "but I didn't take it seriously for about nine months." I meant it as something of a joke, but it comes out too seriously, and my dad nods.

"I know you didn't."

"Why are you so for it?" I ask, curious more than anything else. "If we move to West Virginia, we'll be even farther away from you."

"Not if I move with you," my dad quips. "If you'll have me, that is."

He sounds as serious as he did before, when he mentioned the same thing, except then I thought it was somewhat of a joke. Now I'm not so sure.

"Dad," I ask, "would you really do that? I mean, would you want to?"

"One last adventure in my old age?" he returns, eyes glinting, his mouth curving up into a playful smile. "Why not?"

"Seriously—"

He drops the teasing expression. "I am serious," he says, and I know he means it, which causes me a thrill of both excitement and longing. To have my dad live with us... I never even considered it in Princeton. There's not enough space, and I thought he was happy enough in his little condo. But if we bought a big enough place, he could be with us all the time. The kids would love it, I know, and my dad would be so happy...

"That would be great, Dad," I say, and my dad's smile turns soft and a little weepy as he silently reaches over and squeezes my hand.

A few minutes later, Josh ambles over to us. Even though I've barely seen him all weekend, I can't deny how relaxed he seems, how utterly in his element he is. He looks younger somehow, and more... joyful. "I thought we could go to the church service before the last speaker," he says.

"Church service?" I didn't even know there was one, although it doesn't really surprise me. There's definitely something of a God vibe at this place, which I found I've liked. I grew up going to Sunday School, even if I dropped off in high school, as so many people probably do. Occasionally Josh and I brought the kids to whatever church we landed on for Christmas Eve or Easter, and sometimes afterwards we made noises about how nice it was, and how we should go more often, but never did.

"Yeah," Josh says now, looking a little sheepish. "It just feels right somehow."

"Okay," I say, because I kind of know what he means.

The church service is in one of the big barn-like buildings on the fairground site, and the space is warmed with electric heaters, which is a plus. Bethany and William are bemused but willing about the idea of going to church, Jack is reluctant because he'll have to sit still for an hour or so, and Rose is excited, because she's been excited about basically everything since we got here.

This church service, though, isn't like any other we've been to, all dusty pews and plodding hymns. As we walk in—five minutes late, per usual—the thousand-strong congregation is raising the roof to a worship band that has a drum set, an electric guitar, and a guy on a fiddle who is making it sing.

Once again, I find I am smiling.

Josh joins in with singing numbers I'm positive he's never heard before, while Willian and Bethany, looking frozen with teenaged anxiety, barely mouth the words. Jack is air drumming with a pair of coffee stirrers he grabbed on the way in, and Rose is dancing in her seat. Such is our family.

I catch my dad's eye, and he winks at me before he starts singing himself. Then so do I.

Later, after an inspiring talk on how it takes community to be self-sufficient—not the oxymoron it sounds like—Josh is getting the kids lunch at a hog roast food stand, and I find myself telling him I'll be back in a few minutes. Josh nods, like he knows where I'm going, even though I don't. I've been enjoying this weekend so much, this time with my family, that I'm not sure why I feel the need to go off by myself, only that I do. Maybe it's the sense that a momentous decision is lurking on the horizon, coming closer with every second that passes.

I wander down various paths through the fairground, past tents that are empty and ones that have already been broken down. The convention is about to end, and it saddens, scares, and excites me all at once, because...

What's next?

It's time to make a decision. I know Josh won't pressure me into it, even if he's eager to know what we're doing with the rest of our lives, just as I am, but I feel the need to decide all the same. We can't keep living in this limbo; it's not good for anyone. We've got to go down this road all the way or get off it completely.

So which one?

At the end of a path there is a small wooden building with one side open to the air; it isn't until I step inside that I realize what it is—a little chapel. Small, plain, with rough-hewn backless benches and a cross at the front made of two pine logs. I sink onto a bench near the front, let the peace of the place trickle through me. My thoughts are like minnows darting through my mind, flashes of silver I can't catch hold of. And so I simply sit, absorbing the solitude, letting it strengthen me.

A million memories slip through me, as fast and flashing as my thoughts. I picture the day we bought our house, proud and terrified homeowners at the ripe old age of twenty-eight. The mortgage had felt so enormous, the figures too frightening— with their many zeroes— to contemplate for too long. I remember bringing William home just a few years later; Bethany, at three years old, had burst into tears when we'd told her he was a boy.

I recall boisterous family dinners around the table, the children chasing Max as a puppy in the backyard, the Christmas tree filling up half the family room because Josh insisted on cutting down a huge tree himself—I realize he must have had a homesteader instinct, even then—and countless rainy afternoons playing card games, snow days watching the drifts pile up, summer evenings out on the patio as the fireflies winked in the dusky air.

A sigh escapes me. This feels like an end as well as a beginning.

In the distance, I can hear the sounds of the crowd—laughter, shouting, the occasional thwack of a hammer or roar of a truck as vendors break down their stalls and haul them away. Then I hear another sound—footsteps on the concrete floor of the chapel. I turn, and my breath comes out in a rush as I see who has just slipped into the chapel.

Sarah Walker.

Chapter Twenty

For a second, Sarah doesn't see me, she just slips into the chapel and onto a bench in the back where she slumps, a sigh that *almost* sounds like a sob escaping her. She so clearly thinks she's alone that I'm not sure whether I should make my presence known or not. I debate whether I can pull off pretending I didn't notice her, when she sees me and lets out an embarrassed little laugh.

"Sorry, I thought I was alone. I didn't mean to disturb you."

"No, no," I say quickly. "I was just..." I trail off with an embarrassed laugh to match hers. "Just catching my breath, I guess."

She looks tired, with shadows under her eyes, her face pale with strain, but she smiles and seems to rally, remarking, "I think I recognize you from the first-timer orientation?"

"Yes, we're newbies," I confirm. I feel like I am talking to a celebrity and another, ordinary mom at the same time. And why does she look so tired, and even sad? "We're not even homesteaders, not yet."

Sarah raised her eyebrows. "Not yet?"

"Well... it's certainly something we're thinking about." I pause and then admit in a rush, "To be honest, I've been the one dragging my feet about it all."

Sarah nods in understanding, seeming unsurprised. "It's a demanding life for a woman, especially a wife and mother. The man goes out and beats his chest in the woods, and meanwhile we're in the kitchen, making soup."

I can't help but laugh. "Is that what it really feels like?"

"Sometimes," she admits frankly, and then looks away.

"We've watched your family videos," I am compelled to confess even though saying as much makes me cringe a little bit. *Fangirl alert!* "I know a video can make everything seem fun and amazing, and so I did watch them with a grain of salt, as it were, but... your family seems wonderful."

Sarah's expression lightens as her eyes crinkle in a smile. "They are," she agrees firmly, "but that doesn't make life easy all the time." She runs a hand through her faded blond hair, a soft sigh escaping her, and then asks, "What about you? What's made you drag your feet about homesteading?"

"Leaving everything behind, mostly," I reply after a moment. "We live the typical suburban life, and... I'm *used* to it. Although over the last year, as we've been thinking about doing something different, that has mattered less. And there's a lot that I find exciting and compelling about choosing a way of life that connects you with your family and community, as well as the land." I duck my hand, feeling self-conscious, like I'm an impostor, talking about homesteading in this way. "But then it also feels so unfamiliar and frightening and strange... and I get scared. Scared of making the wrong choice."

Sarah nods slowly. "I can understand that, but the only wrong choice, in my mind, is not making one at all," she says. "You can always learn from your mistakes, but you can't learn from a place of stasis."

"That's very true." I fall silent, thoughts rolling through me, one after the other. "In a way, we've been in stasis this last year," I confess slowly. "Not moving forward with our current life, at least not in a meaningful way, but not taking steps toward something else, either."

"Stasis is comfortable," Sarah says in agreement. "But it can also get incredibly discouraging, because eventually you have to come to terms with the fact that you're going nowhere."

I let out a short laugh of surprised recognition. "Yes, that's exactly it," I admit. "We came to this convention mainly to get more information, but I think also to make a decision. And now the convention is over, and we have to make it." I pause. "*I* have to make it."

"*You* do?" Sarah asks, cocking her head, waiting for more.

"Yes… because I'm pretty sure everyone else has already decided," I say slowly. "My husband Josh is certainly ready to pull the trigger. And I think all our kids might be, too."

"So is anything holding you back besides the fear of making the wrong choice?" Sarah asks gently.

I swallow hard. For nearly a year, I've come up against this nameless, formless fear, time and time again, and I've never gotten past it. I've never even tried; it's just been an immovable barrier smack down in front of me, seemingly impossible to navigate.

"I think…" I begin slowly, feeling out the words, "that I don't actually know." I stare at her in something like wonder. "Isn't that strange? I don't even *know* what I'm afraid of." The realization is both a relief and a weight—after all my protestations, is it really true that the only thing I'm fearing is fear itself? Hello, Franklin Roosevelt.

"The thing about homesteading," Sarah says after a moment, her gaze turning distant, "is that there are no distractions from yourself. There's plenty to do—*so* much to do, hard, demanding, *relentless* stuff to do." She lets out a soft laugh. "The work never ends, and I mean that literally. But in the midst of it all... you come face to face with yourself in a way that is ultimately both good and humbling, but also hard and scary." She trains her gaze back on me, and there is both a shrewdness and compassion in it.

"Because you can't hide behind the mindless busyness of suburban life," she continues, "where you're rushing here and there but you're not actually *accomplishing* anything, or at least you don't feel as if you are. And you can't hide behind the mindless scrolling on social media or the fact that everyone is the same as you, too busy to do anything that feels meaningful."

Ouch. I swallow hard, unable to reply, because I relate to every word.

"Somehow," Sarah continues thoughtfully, "when it's just you and the land or the cow or the fence post you're trying to dig, you face your limitations and weaknesses in a way you never have to in what you think of as real life." She gives me a smile of wry frankness. "If you want to find out who and what you really are, if you want to face your weaknesses and fears and be forced to deal with them... then definitely homestead." She subsides with both a smile and sigh.

"Wow." I find I have to clear my throat. "Thanks for the advice."

Sarah's smile is tinged with something like sorrow as she rises from her bench. "My pleasure. This talk cleared my head, so thank you, but I should go find my family now." She gives me a wave of farewell before slipping out of the chapel before I have a chance to ask her anything about herself—or wonder why at times she looked so weary and sounded so sad. I wonder if I'll ever find out. If we end up homesteading, will we see the Walkers again? Somehow I feel like we might.

I've been gone for nearly half an hour, so after Sarah leaves I rise myself, and head back to the picnic tables by the food stands where the kids are working their way through their pulled pork and apple sauce. A lot of the vendors have already left along with the attendees, and the place is starting to feel empty and a little desolate.

Josh looks up as I approach. "Had a little think?" he asks with a knowing smile.

"Yes..."

"And?" Bethany asks, her voice sharpening.

I turn to look at her, bemused. "And what?"

"Mom, you must know that you're the one who gets to decide," Bethany tells me in the well-duh tone children, especially teenaged ones, are so good at.

"Why me?" I ask, both curious and amused.

"Because," Bethany says in even more of a well-duh tone, "the rest of us have already decided."

Slowly, surprised even though I admitted as much to Sarah, I look around at all my children. "Have you?" I ask, and four young heads nod solemnly at me, jolting me further. I knew they were leaning that way, but maybe not quite this much. "All of you really want to move to West Virginia—or wherever—and homestead?" I ask, like a test they have to pass.

"Yes, Mom," William exclaims, sounding exasperated. "Why are you so surprised?"

"And you, Dad?" I ask my father, and he laughs.

"Abby, you know what I think."

"And you know what *I* think," Josh chimes in, giving me a smile full of affection. "So you don't even need to ask."

So it really is my decision... and yet how can I make it? It still feels too huge, too strange, too scary.

"How would we even do this?" I burst out. "I mean, *if* I said yes..."

"Well." Josh's eyes dance as a smile tugs at his mouth. "There's a property in West Virginia I've been looking at that we could see today. It's about three hours west of here."

"So the exact opposite direction of where we're going," I point out, but I am smiling too.

Josh shrugs, as unfazed as ever. "Pretty much."

"How do you know we could see it today?"

"I might have called while you were having your walkabout," Josh admits.

"Dad said you needed some thinking time," Jack tells me with a grin. "And you did!"

"I did," I confirm. I don't know how I feel about all my thoughts yet, but... "And this property you've been looking at? What's it like?"

"Seven acres in a valley twenty miles southeast of Buckholt, which is a cute little town in the middle of the state." He starts scrolling on his phone. "Do you want to see it?"

I hold my hand out. Josh swipes a few times and then hands me the phone while the kids crowd around, eager for a look. I look at the details first—seven acres, three bedrooms, one bathroom, and a price tag of an astonishing one hundred and sixty-five thousand dollars. You couldn't get a shed for that much in Princeton.

Silently I start to swipe. Inside, the house is neat, if well-worn and small. The living room has an impressive stone fireplace and a picture window overlooking a wildflower meadow, which are definitely two pluses. There's a wraparound porch, but no rocking chairs. Instead it's filled with firewood. The bedrooms, which the children would have to share, are much smaller than the ones they currently have. The kitchen and bathroom look like a throwback to the 1970s, filled with avocado-green appliances. The place needs some serious TLC. I swallow hard.

Do I really want to do this? Do the kids?

"You'd have to share bedrooms," I tell them, like a warning. William and Jack share now, but their bedroom is three times the size of the ones in the photos.

"We'd remodel, of course," Josh says hurriedly. "The price is so cheap we could afford to do it pretty much right away. Expand the porch and the living room, add two new bedrooms and a bathroom, bump out the kitchen..."

Remodeling could very well be a nightmare, as well as take forever. I swipe again, and I feel myself start to soften a little more at the photos of the outside. Two barns and a chicken coop, all looking slightly worse for wear but still standing. No vegetable garden, but certainly the space for one, and a little hill, verdant green, rolling down to a sweet little pond fringed by birch trees. There's a dock and a raft and a mossy rock jutting out over the water. It looks like something out of a children's story.

"Of the seven acres," Josh continues quietly, like he's worried he might scare me off, "they've cleared four. The other three are woodland, behind that pond. There's also a well and septic tank, both in good working order. We could look into getting solar panels to be completely off-grid."

Off-grid. A concept that I'd never thought seriously about, if at all, before. Am I really thinking this way now? I shake my head slowly in disbelief, but my family takes it as negation.

"Mom..." William protests softly and Rose silently take my hand.

Then I look up. I hand the phone back to my husband, a new resolve firing through me. "All right," I say. "Let's go take a look."

Chapter Twenty-One

The drive to near Buckholt, West Virginia, feels endless. The kids jabber the whole time, about the workshops they attended but also about the house they seem to think we are definitely going to buy. Rose is already figuring out where the cat bed will go, and Bethany is swiping through photos of the property on her phone, planning out her herb garden. Jack wants a shooting range, and William is considering the pros and cons of having more than one cow, which my dad listens to in his equable way, pointing out how much longer the milking would take. The workshops have clearly rubbed off on him.

Yet how is this my family? I feel both bemused and excited, and still deeply apprehensive. I may have jumped off, but I haven't landed yet.

Josh reaches across the seat to give my knee a reassuring squeeze. "We're just looking," he says.

I nod back to the kids; my dad serenely sitting in the midst of them, a faint smile on his face as they talk his ear off. "You know it's already bigger than that," I tell Josh.

"I'm excited they're excited," he replies with a wry smile. "Somehow I don't think we'd be experiencing this energy if we were talking about moving to the Falkland Islands."

I laugh in memory. "Maybe Buckholt, West Virginia is your Falkland Islands."

"Twenty miles outside of Buckholt, West Virginia," Josh reminds me. "But maybe it is."

"So how far do we have to drive to get a gallon of milk?" I quip, only to have William groan from behind me.

"Only to the backyard, Mom, because we'll have our own milk cow."

I slap my forehead, laughing. "Sorry, I forgot. How far to the nearest pizza place, then?"

"Mom, read the room," Bethany admonishes me, smiling. "We'll make our own pizza. Didn't you learn how to make mozzarella this weekend?"

"It was yummy," Rose chimes in.

I just laugh and shake my head. My children's—and my husband's, *and* my dad's—excitement is infectious, and for once I'm not going to be the pragmatic, practical one tethering everybody else, Josh especially, to mundane reality. Right now, I want to run with it, and so I do.

It's overcast and bitterly cold as we pull up to the house on County Road. We've been driving for about ten miles without seeing anything but rolling meadowland and deep forest, with the occasional farm or house barely able to be glimpsed through the wilderness, a flash of roof or red shingle.

Josh had said the house was in a valley, and it really was. We had to drive down a narrow road that wound its way through the dense trees to the bottom of the valley, passing several houses and farms nestled into the hillside, and then over an alarmingly narrow iron bridge that spanned a rushing river, chucks of ice bobbing in its forceful current, before going up again, the road practically doubling back on itself as it continued to wind its way through the woods. Finally we found the place, in its own little clearing and built into a hill, surrounded by a forest of maples and oaks, birches and beech, the nearest neighbor no more than a glimpse of roof farther down a rutted dirt road. I wondered who they might be, and if they'd be neighborly.

As I stepped out of the car, the isolation felt immense—both wonderful and frightening. The only sound was the wind soughing through the bare branches high above us, with a whispery rattle. Distant in the sky I glimpsed what had to be a hawk, judging by its elegant and enormous wingspan, soaring over the river now far below us.

We would definitely not be popping out to Target here. I'd already checked; the nearest Target was over sixty miles away. But beyond that... beyond that one glimpse of roof, I couldn't see any other houses from the driveway, although we had passed a few places along the way. I told myself it wasn't that different than our house back in New Jersey; yes, we could see our neighbors there, but we hardly ever interacted with them. Hopefully, whoever lived near us in this wild, little valley would be welcoming to greenhorns.

That is, if we were actually thinking of *buying* this place.

"Is the realtor meeting us here?" I ask Josh.

"She said she'd try to get here, but the key is under the mat, and we could help ourselves."

I let out a guffaw of disbelief. That definitely would not happen in New Jersey. "Seriously?"

"Seriously," Josh confirms with a grin. "Abby, it's different in the sticks."

"I guess it is."

The kids have all clambered out of the car and are eagerly exploring; Bethany is pacing out the cleared area to the left of the house that borders the woods, while William is peeking into one of the two barns, both of which look sturdy enough but in need of some TLC, as does the house. My dad and Jack have gone off to have a look at the pond. Rose smiles up at me.

"This seems like a nice place for a cat."

I glance at the house, with its low, rambling roof leading to a peaked gable, the chimney made of what look like local stones, the round wooden posts of the porch. "It does," I agree, and reach for her hand. Josh climbs the rickety steps to the porch and looks under the mat. There is the key, just as promised. It almost feels magical, like a fairy tale come to life, the house, dilapidated as it is, waiting for us.

He picks it up and fits it into the lock, then turns back to me. "Ready?" he asks, and it feels like he's asking about so much more than this house.

"Ready," I reply, and squeeze Rose's hand.

Josh turns the key and opens the door. He stands aside so I step in first, breathing in dust and mildew and possibility. The living room would feel small save for the fireplace and the picture window overlooking the hill sloping down the pond.

"In the spring, apparently it's covered in wildflowers," Josh says from behind me. "That's the unofficial name of this area—Wildflower Valley."

I try to picture it, although now everything is brown and iron-hard. Beneath me the floorboards squeak and as I take a step one sags alarmingly.

"Remodel," Josh whispers, and I nod.

Are we really doing this?

Still holding Rose's hand, I walk through the rooms—living room, kitchen, bathroom in 1970s avocado green, and three small bedrooms. Up a flight of rickety, narrow stairs, there is an attic room, with a low, sloping ceiling and two dormer windows.

I stoop to look through one of the windows and see the glint of the pond in the distance. It's frozen over, its surface a smooth sweep of ice. William is tossing rocks on it, no doubt to test whether it's thick enough to walk on; Jack is pulling my dad's hand, desperate to try the ice.

I walk downstairs to inspect the rest—a basement, dark and damp, with a separate pantry whose door I have to steel myself to open, in case there are spiders or rats, or goodness knows what else. There aren't—there are just wooden shelves, worn with use, waiting to be stacked with mason jars. I run my hand along one, come away with a palm full of dust.

Upstairs again, I check out the mudroom that leads to the backdoor; the small space is crammed with an ancient washing machine and dryer, the floor caked with mud from a lifetime of tramping inside in work boots. There is history to this place, along with hope.

Josh doesn't say a word as I inspect everything; he just silently waits for my verdict. I am trying to capture his vision—the side of the house facing the valley built onto, doubling the size of the living room, adding two bedrooms and another bathroom. The kitchen expanded to the back porch, which is built on stilts over the hill. It would be a lot of work, and part of me would just rather buy a bigger, readymade home for five times as much, but... if we go for a house like this, Josh can quit his job. We could live on the proceeds from our house for two or three years, making do with my salary and health coverage.

And, I know, I want that for him. He's provided for our family in a job he's never liked—something I knew but pretended I didn't—for twenty years. It really is time for a change.

"Let's look outside," I say.

Our breath comes out in frosty puffs as we walk around the house to inspect the outbuildings. One barn has garage doors, and inside it looks like it was used as a workshop of sorts. The second barn has a stall for our milk cow—yes, I really am thinking that way—as well as a tack room and a space to store hay.

I have never milked a cow in my life, no one in our family has, but... we could learn? Maybe?

"Let's walk down to the pond," I say.

The frost-tipped grass crunches under our feet as the sky darkens at its edges and dusk draws in, turning the horizon a pearly pink. The boys are still at the pond; they've now ventured onto the ice, which thankfully is thick enough to stand on. They're both delighted, jumping up and down, sliding along as best as they can in their sneakers.

When we move here, I think, *we'll have to get ice skates.*

Then I realize I thought when, not if. And *then* I realize I have been thinking *when* not *if* since we first stepped on this property. Something about this place has already settled in my bones. Never mind the small bedrooms, the mildew in the basement, the fact that it's so quiet my ears ring and the isolation scares me—for *now*.

It still feels right.

On the worn path to the pond, I turn to Josh. "What do you think?"

He takes the question seriously, although I can see the excitement in his eyes, the way his fingers drum against his thigh. "I think it has possibilities," he says carefully, and I laugh aloud.

"Come on, Josh, be honest. You love it."

He grins, both abashed and ebullient. "All right, yes, I love it. I love that the kids can run around and be free, I love that we have space for a garden and a cow and chickens and solar panels and whatever else we want. I love the thought of being a family here, all of us together, all the time."

"And that doesn't scare you?" I ask, half joking, half serious. "The 'all the time' part?"

"Well, yes, a little bit," he admits. "But I don't *want* it to scare me, Abby. Why should either of us be scared of spending time with our kids? Isn't this what we wanted, when we first had them? Isn't this what we were *made* for?"

"You sound like one of those workshops," I murmur, even though I agree with him.

Sarah, I'm pretty sure, was right. When you homestead, you have to face yourself and all your fears. Confront all your weaknesses. Deal with all your shortcomings. And yet isn't that what anyone should *want* to do in life? Not just skate by on the surface—not just of things, but of yourself.

"This is only the first house we've seen," I tell Josh, like a warning. "There might be other properties that are way more suitable."

"There might be," he agrees, and yet I think we both know it doesn't matter. This place has something about it.

"Wildflower Valley..." I muse. "Do you think the neighbors are nice?"

"I think we'll find out."

I shake my head. "When you first asked me for that ice cream, I had no idea what I was getting into."

He laughs as he reaches for me, slipping his arms around my waist to draw me close. "And isn't that the best part?" he asks. "The not knowing? The wonder?"

"Arguable," I tease, "but maybe."

I rest my head against his shoulder, savoring the sweetness of the moment, just as Rose runs over to tug at my hand and Jack comes sprinting up from the pond, followed more slowly by William.

"We're buying this place, right?" Jack asks eagerly as he skids to a stop.

"And we're getting a cat!" Rose chimes in, a statement rather than a question.

William and Bethany both join us from further afield, and my father follows behind at an amble.

For the first time, I don't feel afraid. The unknown still looms in front of us, as mysterious as ever, but also exciting.

"Well..." I begin, just as we hear the sound of a car coming up the road, the engine cutting, and then a car door slam.

"Hellooo?" a woman calls. "I'm Wendy Miller, the realtor? Can I show you around?"

I meet Josh's gaze, and then my dad's and my children's, and we all start to laugh.

Chapter Twenty-Two

Everything seems to happen very quickly after that. Wendy, the realtor, walks us through the property, showing us all the things we'd already noticed and pointing out a few more—a root cellar dug into the hillside and a little orchard of apple and plum trees on the far side of the barn, twisted and bare, but I can already imagine them laden with fruit. She mentions the neighbors—the Hewsons live in the house whose roof I glimpsed further down the road; they're retired, having moved from Richmond, Virginia to embrace the rural life six years ago.

"Very friendly," she says firmly. "I always buy their honey at the farmer's market in Buckholt."

"*Bees...*" my dad murmurs, and I can already see him in the full beekeeper regalia, standing in front of a hive.

We head back to New Jersey with promises to be in touch soon, although Wendy admits that no one has so much as viewed the place in weeks. There's no rush on her side, but we still feel the need to make a decision, to get *going*, and so, a week after we've been to the house, we put in an offer and learn the next day it has been accepted. Josh calls our own realtor, and our house goes on sale the same day. I start to panic.

First I panic about packing all our stuff—only about half our furniture will fit into the new house—and then about living through a remodel, because Josh wants to move by March so we can plant for the summer.

"*March*!" I yelp. "But then Bethany won't even graduate—"

"I don't care," Bethany says quickly. "I can get a GED or whatever."

This is not reassuring. "A high school diploma is important, Bethany—"

"She can finish online, through a cyber school," Josh says, like he has an answer to everything. "I've already looked into it."

Thinking about Bethany's education makes me remember that if we do this, I'm meant to be *homeschooling* my other three kids. Something I conveniently forgot about when thinking about homesteading.

"I'm going to be Exhibit A for why they should have stricter laws about homeschooling," I tell Josh one evening when I've been browsing homeschool curriculum sites and getting more and more freaked out. "There's no way I can teach them everything. Rose is going to get to the age of fifteen and not know how to tell time."

"Well," Josh replies affably, "there are worse things than not knowing how to tell time."

"That kind of attitude is not helping," I practically snap. The nearest high school is thirty miles away; homeschooling really is the most reasonable option, especially if we want all the together time we've been talking about. But is it really feasible? For me, or my kids?

Josh drops his smile, giving me an earnest look instead. "I'm serious, Abby. Part of doing this is rethinking our whole approach—to everything. Why does education need to be what some faceless bureaucratic organization decides it is—six hours in a classroom, learning a certain set of predetermined facts?"

"Now you're really not helping," I warn him. "I'm not about to become some off-grid anti-establishment prepper, Josh." I wag my finger at him. "I can get on board with a lot of things, but let's not throw the baby out with the bathwater. There's a reason why kids go to school, and I am never going to be the kind of mom who turns a trip to the grocery store into an algebra class." As did one chirpy mom I watched, my heart sinking, on an Instagram reel. Spare me the zealots.

Josh holds up both his hands. "Okay, okay," he soothes. "Just have an open mind to it all, Abby, and remember, I can help. Your dad, too." My dad is planning to sell his condo and move in with us, hopefully by the fall, when the remodel is, also hopefully, finished. "You are definitely not doing this all alone," Josh insists.

"Okay." It is somewhat comforting to think that Josh will be there to do some of the heavy lifting; we decided, after our offer was accepted, that he would quit his job while I would continue part-time remotely. I still craved the security blanket of an income and sense of purpose, while Josh wanted full liberation, although he did reassure me that he could return to work if he needed to. And having my dad around will be great for all of us, I remind myself. This is definitely scary, but it can still work.

In any case, I know the thing I am really panicking about is that we are doing this at all. We've set it all in motion and everything seems to be happening faster and faster. Josh has been on the phone to various builders and plumbers; I've notified the kids' schools and our circle of friends. Josh called his parents, who were bemused by the notion, to say the least, and I met my brother in New York for dinner to tell him; he thought we were downright crazy.

"What, you're preparing for Armageddon?" he joked, and I managed a laugh.

"No, just trying to live differently." It was a refrain I clung to, to keep this from feeling too weird.

The kids, at least, remain enthusiastic, although I know they, like Josh and me, will have their setbacks and slumps at some point. It's too much change to sail through unscathed, although at the moment that's what it feels like for them. They pack up their rooms and say goodbye to their friends without much angst at all.

"We're all ready for this," Josh assures me when I worry about whether they're not processing this enough. "We've been thinking about it for a year."

"I know, but... actually doing it feels different, for *all* of us."

"It feels good," Josh insists gently. "I'm not saying it's going to be smooth sailing forever, but let's enjoy the easy times while we have them, okay?"

"Okay," I relent, because that makes sense. And like Josh said, the hard times we'll come... and we'll face them together.

Still, it's bittersweet to know I'm spending the last few weeks in the place where I was first married, had children, became a grownup. I drive down familiar roads with a sense of nostalgia; even the notorious traffic on Route 1 doesn't bother me the way it used to.

I don't have a lot of time to wallow in sentiment, though, because there is so much to *do*. We haven't moved yet, but we still have to make plans. A lot of plans. Josh and I spend every evening poring over various online catalogues—seeds, tools, chickens, cows. I insist we can't start with everything at once, especially if we're remodeling the house, as well.

"Let's just add one thing at a time," I plead with him. "Rather than buy a whole barnyard of animals at the beginning."

"Well, we have to start with *something*," Josh argues, and I know he'd be happy to do it all right now—have the laying chickens as well as the meat ones, cows and pigs and who knows what else. Fortunately, my husband still knows how to see sense, and he agrees to wait until we've moved and settled—how long that takes remains to be seen—before we start adding to our livestock.

An offer is made on our house and accepted in mid-February for over the asking price. The buyers want to move as soon as possible, and our house in Wildflower Valley is ready and waiting for us already, so there's no time to waste. It feels as if life is speeding up, the days a blur as we cull our possessions—seventeen years in the same house has given us a *lot* of junk—and make plans to move. Max, sensing the change, starts to follow me around so closely I regularly trip over him. We hire a moving truck and have several last rounds of goodbyes.

"I can't believe you're really doing this," Kerry exclaims as she hugs me at my very last book club meeting. I still didn't manage to read the book.

"I kind of can't either," I admit.

"You know I'm actually a little envious?" she admits with a shaky little laugh. "I mean, it sounds like such an adventure. And so much of life just feels like the same thing, day after day..."

"My days are going to be pretty samey," I reply, as much to myself as her. "Doing all the homesteady chores and stuff." Even if I don't entirely know what those are yet. I'll learn. We all will.

"Still..." She shakes her head slowly. "Let me know how it goes, okay? Keep in touch."

"I promise." I have a feeling I might keep in touch with Kerry more from West Virginia than I did living half a dozen miles away.

And then the day comes—the tenth of March, bright blue sky, the air still crisp and wintry. The moving truck arrives at eight o'clock in the morning, while I'm packing a crate of last-minute supplies to tide us over until we can unpack all the boxes.

"I can't believe we're actually doing this," Bethany says as she comes into the kitchen. "It's so surreal."

"I know." After spending a year dithering and dreaming, the actual *doing* does feel surreal. And scary. And exciting. I am trying to ride all the emotions without letting them freak me out. Max sticks close to my ankles as I liberate Rose's worn blue teddy bear from the tangle of her sheets; she'd had it since she was a baby, and I do not want to be searching for it in boxes tonight.

I add it to the crate of supplies, along with our coffee pot, our passports and other important documents, Max's dog food and water bowl, and my favorite mug. William puts his travel chessboard in, and I raise my eyebrow at him.

"Do you really think we'll have time to play chess today?"

He shrugs, smiling. "Maybe tonight." I picture it, with us all tucked up in front of that beautiful stone fireplace, and I smile.

The movers are ruthlessly efficient, lugging our stuff out the front door and into their truck with cheerful indifference. Amazingly, by noon everything is packed up and the house is empty save for dust bunnies and the detritus that had been living under the sofa for longer than I care to consider.

"*That's* where my AirPods went!" Bethany exclaims, swooping down to snatch the earbuds she lost over a year ago.

Together we all walk through the empty house, room by room, making sure there's nothing else that needs to be taken, but it's all gone.

The kids, impatient now, bored with empty rooms, head out to the car, while I stand by the kitchen window and gaze out at the yard one last time. How many times have I stood here—washing dishes, preparing food, daydreaming or worrying or just waking up? My life played out by the kitchen sink, day by day and moment by moment.

Josh joins me, putting his arm around my shoulder. I lean into him, and neither of us speaks for a minute.

"It's been a good life," he finally says quietly, and I nod, a lump forming in my throat. Even though I am excited for this next chapter—and I *am*, finally—I'm also sad to be closing this one. I've accepted that I can feel both at once, and it's okay. Goodbyes are almost always hard.

Max whines by the door, more anxious than ever. The moving truck has already left, trundling down the road with all our possessions. The car is packed, the kids are ready. It's a six-and-a-half-hour drive to our new home, and we want to get there before the movers do.

It's time to go.

I turn away from the kitchen window and slip my hand into Josh's. Together we step out of our house and into our new life—whatever that looks like.

"Hey," Jack calls from the backseat as we walk to the car. "What took you so long?"

It's a good question, I reflect as I slide into the passenger seat and Josh gets behind the wheel. What *did* take me so long? Nameless fears and worries, clinging to safety or really, what was just known. Well, none of it matters now, because we are, finally, for better or worse, on our way. All of us, together, jumping in feet first.

As Josh pulls out of the driveway, I turn back to smile at our children crowded in the back two seats; Rose has her teddy bear tucked up in her arm, Jack is already starting to fidget, William is gazing out the window, looking a little morose now that we're actually leaving, and Bethany is scrolling on her phone.

This is definitely going to be a journey, I think, and not just a physical one. For all of us.

"When are we going to get there?" Rose asks before we've even turned on the main road.

"Can we stop at Starbucks?" Bethany chimes in.

Max, lying at William's feet, lets out a whine of anxiety at all this change.

Josh glances at me askance, as if he's afraid I might already do a tailspin into doubt at these little blips, but I just laugh.

"Let's just get going," I say to everyone, "and then we'll see."

It feels like a life motto at the moment, and one I am intending to live by. No more panicking, or worrying, or wondering whether we made the right choice.

We did it, and now, at long last, it's time to begin.

As Josh turns onto the highway to head west across Pennsylvania, I realize I can't wait.

Find out how the Bryant family adapts to their new homesteading life in the next book in the series, *Both Feet In*, out May 15, 2025.

Enjoyed *Leap of Faith*? There's more to discover! Find out about Kate's other books on her website https://katehewittbooks.com/

Dear Reader,

Thank you so much for reading *Leap of Faith*, and I really hope you enjoyed adventuring along with the Bryants! I was inspired to write this series after I'd written another, very different kind of homesteading book, *The Last Stars in the Sky*, which follows a family as they learn to homestead after a nuclear holocaust. While many people loved the dystopian element in that novel, other people preferred the focus on homesteading, and so I thought, *why not write a story about a family learning to homestead, but without the nuclear war?!*

I've always had a fascination with the homesteading life. When I was four years old, my parents bought 100 acres on a private lake in rural Ontario and enacted their own homesteading dream. While it wasn't off-grid living, it was certainly remote—20 miles from the nearest town, with no TV, wifi, and only a party phone line. My parents had a huge garden, potato and cornfields, and also made maple syrup every spring. In the winter, we had to snowmobile to the cottage down a quarter-mile of unplowed dirt road. Looking back, I'm amazed my dad let me drive the snowmobile when I was only five years old! I'm so grateful that I got to be part of my parents' adventures, and that my children did, too. I only wished we'd had chickens...

While researching homesteading for this series, I read countless books, watched many YouTube videos, and subscribed to several homesteading magazines. I am not, however, a true homesteader—not yet, anyway—so any inaccuracies or errors as the Bryants bumble their way through homesteading come from my own inexperience, which I am always looking to rectify.

In the meantime, I hope you enjoyed learning along with the Bryants, and celebrating the importance of family, nature, and learning to be resourceful and resilient. There are lots more adventures planned, and you can preorder the second book in the series, *Both Feet In*. You can also learn more about the Wildflower Valley Books, buy them direct as well as Wildflower Valley merchandise on the website: http://www.wildflower-valley.com

Happy Reading,

Kate

P.S. Turn the page to read the first chapter of *Both Feet In*, the second book in the series!

Both Feet In

Book Two

Chapter One

Predictably, we run into problems just five minutes after we arrive. I was expecting some kind of snag, but I'd hoped we'd have ten minutes, at least, maybe fifteen, before we began to seriously rethink this madcap plan.

Not that anyone was actually doing that. Yet. We'd just driven six hours from Princeton, New Jersey to Wildflower Valley, West Virginia, on something of a high, fueled by Starbucks ('last chance for a latte, guys!') and giddy excitement that we were finally doing this.

Six weeks ago, we decided as a family, to pack in our suburban lives, both frantic and mundane, for homesteading in the country. It took my husband Josh over a year to convince me that this might be a not-so-terrible idea, as well as a few crises along the way that forced me to rethink my priorities as a mother, a wife, a person. Suburban life wasn't working any of for us anymore, with its myriad pressures and problems. All of us—Josh, me, our four children and even my dad—wanted something different. Something that involved chickens and tomato plants and living 'slower'. So here we are.

Wildflower Valley is in central West Virginia, an area of serene mountain lakes and the rugged peaks of the Appalachians cutting into the horizon, thirty miles from the tiny town of Buckholt, and having just four other residents—that we know of, anyway—nestled on the slopes that are named for the colorful flowers that dot its meadows—I hope—in the spring. In early March, however, the landscape is comprised entirely of stark, leafless trees stretching skeletal branches to a steel-gray sky, dead, brown grass... and mud. Lots of mud, frozen into deep ruts but soft and sludgy in the middle, as we discovered when driving through it, with Josh valiantly going into lower and lower gear as our minivan heaved and groaned in protest.

Our little house, subject to an imminent expansion, is perched halfway up one side of the valley, with its own tiny orchard, barn, and a sweet little pond fringed by birches out back. It's also at the top of a steep and rutted dirt drive, several hundred yards long, winding its way up the hillside. Our minivan made it up with some wheezy protest and a couple of clanks, but we are just climbing out of the car, stretching and trying not to shiver in the wintry weather, when the moving truck that followed us from Princeton pulls to a stop at the bottom of the hill.

"They're here!" Rose, my happy just-turned-seven-year-old, calls excitedly. My other children—Bethany, eighteen, William, fifteen, and Jack, eleven—all stop to watch the truck begin the climb up the hill as our dog Max cowers behind my legs, tail beating the frozen ground, clearly anxious about all the disruption to our lives.

The truck doesn't move. We watch, caught between apprehension and hope, as it idles there for a moment or two at the bottom of the driveway, not even attempting to turn in, and then the driver rolls down the window.

"We're not getting up that hill," he calls up to us, his tone friendly but resolute.

Josh, jovial as ever, strolls down toward the truck, smile firmly in place, eyebrows raised in cheerful expectation. "Shall we give it a try, at least?" he suggests, even though I'm pretty sure there's no we about this situation.

The driver shakes his head, his steely gaze on the steep hill. "Sorry, buddy, but it's not happening. I don't want to get stuck on that incline and roll back down. Not in my contract."

I decide to let my husband handle this one and, with my arm around Rose's shoulder, I shepherd my children inside. "Let's check out the house," I suggest cheerily, turning my back on the moving truck still parked stubbornly at the bottom of the hill.

"What happens if they can't get up the hill?" William asks. He sounds as if he's waiting for further information before he decides whether to worry.

"They'll figure it out," I state more firmly than I feel. The truth is, as excited as I've been to make this move, now that we're here, I'm feeling a little bit overwhelmed. Everything feels so strange—the empty sky, the endless woods, the silence save for the rumble of the moving truck's engine which suddenly cuts off, plunging us into a wintry stillness. That can't be a good sign, I think as I take the key to our house out of my pocket and fit in the door. I turn it, open the door and step inside to our new home, my children crowding in behind me.

For a second, we are all quiet, and I have a feeling we all forgot just how small it is. Of course, we've got tremendous plans for an extension—bumping the kitchen out over the hillside and expanding the living room out front, plus adding two bedrooms and another bathroom onto the side. We've already hired an architect and engaged a building crew, and they're going to start as soon as it's warm enough to live in a house that has one wall more or less open to the air.

But right now... the house feels kind of small and dark and musty, and I have to remind myself that we knew this, that it doesn't actually change anything.

"I forgot how amazing the fireplace is," I exclaim. It is amazing, taking up almost all of one wall, built of rounded stones, now blackened with smoke. I picture blazing fires, with us all happily gathered around, toasting marshmallows or having a read-aloud of some worthy tome, because on top of the whole homesteading thing, we're also homeschooling. Major life changes all around.

"Which bedroom is mine?" Bethany calls as she wanders down the narrow hallway that leads to the three small bedrooms on the side of the house, overlooking the orchard. The other kids follow her, already jockeying for pole position when it comes to bedrooms, even though we'd agreed back in New Jersey who got to sleep where. At least I thought we had.

I leave them to it and walk back to the kitchen, taking in the view over the sink of the gentle hill that rolls down to the little pond fringed with trees. I fell in love with that bucolic sight when we toured the property less than two months ago, but it seems like an age ago now. For the last six weeks, we've been in constant motion—packing, giving away stuff, arranging the planned renovations, figuring out the startling shape of this new life of ours.

The barn, I know, is full of equipment Josh can't wait to figure out how to use. The moving truck at the bottom of the hill has, in addition to all our worldly possessions, stacks of books on how to garden, raise chickens, can vegetables, milk a cow. If it's possible to learn how to homestead from a book alone, then I am certainly covered, but I have a feeling it's going to take more than a little learning. Thankfully, I have the internet, too.

Now I stand by the sink, resting my hands on the cracked enamel, as I keep my gaze on the view of muddy yard, weathered barn, the glimpse of the pond beyond, its surface flat and gray under the wintry sky. I live here, I think, with a thrill of wonder—and a little bit of terror. None of this feels real yet. I can't help but believe my suburban house outside Princeton is waiting for me, even though I put up the sold sign myself, and this is just an Airbnb experience that we might laugh about later, joke about how we roughed it for once.

"Mom!" Jack sprints into the kitchen, skidding to a stop. "I am so not sharing a room with William. He snores."

I breathe in and out. We discussed the sleeping arrangements in detail back in Princeton, when it all seemed theoretical and all four of our children had their own bedrooms, although admittedly Rose's was tiny. But they knew they all had to share here, at least until the renovations were finished, which won't be until the summer. They were all fine with it, back in Princeton. The reality, I know, always feels different.

"Jack." I turn from the view and try to smile. "There are only three bedrooms in this house. You know you have to share, at least for a few months."

"But not with William," Jack protests stubbornly.

I stare at him in amused exasperation. "Who then?"

"Rose—"

"I don't want to share with Jack!" Rose shrieks as she runs into the kitchen. "He's a boy and he smells!"

"I think something died in the closet of my bedroom," Bethany announces as she joins us in the kitchen, which is now feeling pretty crowded. "It smells like roadkill."

"How do you know what roadkill smells like?" Jack demands, and Bethany just shrugs.

"Okay, let's just take a breather from talking about bedrooms, okay?" I suggest. "First we need all our stuff." I strain to hear the hopeful sound of a moving truck laboring up the hill, but all is silence. Max whines, pawing the back door.

"What happens if the moving truck can't get up the hill?" William asks. He's starting to sound worried.

"That's a good question." And one I don't have the answer to, but I hope Josh, my indefatigable husband, does. "Let's cross that bridge when and if we come to it," I tell William. "Shall we look around outside?"

Everyone looks somewhat uncertain about this prospect, and I can't entirely blame them. It's cold and muddy and dusk is already settling over the trees, shadow lengthening across the tufty grass, but this is our life now, and we need to embrace it.

"Come on, guys," I cajole. "Let's get the supplies out of the car, and then we can check out the barn and the pond."

As we troop outside, I tell myself that a few blips are to be expected. I knew the shine would wear off the dream, as it so often does when we're confronted with the mundane and uninspiring aspects of reality. Once we've unpacked and actually started doing things, everything will look and feel better. Even if right now I'm not entirely sure how to start.

Once outside, we unload the boxes of food, dishes, and clothes I packed in the minivan so we wouldn't have to hunt through the many boxes from the moving truck.

I glance toward the bottom of the hill, and see that Josh is still talking to the movers, and is now gesticulating wildly, his arms windmilling through the air. That doesn't seem like a good sign, and so I turn away. If the movers refuse to go up the hill, how we will get our stuff to the house? We can schlep the boxes for sure, but we'll definitely struggle with taking hauling some of the bigger furniture all that way.

It's a problem I decide not to think about now, heeding my own advice about crossing bridges, and so we head back into the kitchen where I unpack the coffeemaker, coffee, and milk for a much-needed cup, and the kids root around for something to eat. Maybe if I offer the movers coffee they'll decide to give the hill a try?

I am just digging out cups for this purpose when Josh comes into the kitchen. His hair is ruffled, his cheeks reddened with cold, and he has a look on his face that I know well. It's the determined smile of someone who is about to give me bad news and act like it's actually good.

"So," he says briskly, planting his hands on his hips. "The movers can't get the truck up the hill."

"Have they tried?" Bethany asks skeptically, and Josh's smile widens a fraction.

"No, but these guys are experienced, and they don't want to get stuck. Understandably."

William comes from the living room to stand in the doorway, his hands jammed in the pockets of his jeans. "So what are they going to do? Can they take all our stuff up the hill themselves?"

"Well..." Josh's smile falters, which alarms me. My husband's inexhaustible cheeriness is legendary. His smile never falters. "Apparently, that's not in their contract."

"What?" This from me, a sharp huff of disbelief. "Seriously?"

He nods, somber now. "Seriously. According to the contract we signed, if they have to walk more than a hundred yards we have to pay extra."

"Okay, then let's pay extra," I say quickly. Problem solved. After all, we need the movers to move. That's what they do, or at least, are meant to do.

Josh grimaces. "Yeah, well, I offered, obviously, but they weren't interested."

"But don't they have to..." I begin, but already he'd shaking his head. "If we didn't specify the hill or the distance in the original contract, they don't have to agree to anything."

Briefly I close my eyes. Okay, so we need to figure out a way to move all our furniture and belongings up a steep hill by ourselves. This doesn't feel doable, but it can be. Hopefully. When I open my eyes, I see that Rose is looking anxious, Jack mutinous, and into the tense silence, Bethany asks what the point of having movers who don't move stuff is, which is exactly the question I'm asking myself. This feels like more than a blip, but we can still deal with it. We will deal with it.

"Okay," I say to Josh, forcing a smile. "So what do you think we should do?" I am thinking about calling another moving company, hire local hardy handymen, something that does not involve us carrying furniture that is way too heavy for us...

My husband flashes back the determinedly bright smile I know and love, but my stomach still swirls with dread, because I already know what he's going to say.

"We move it ourselves, of course."

About the author

Kate Hewitt is the author of many novels of both historical and contemporary fiction. Her novels have been called 'unputdownable' and 'the most emotional book I have ever read' by readers.

An American ex-pat for many years, she now lives in New Jersey with her husband, two of her five children (the others are scattered across the globe!), their two Golden Retrievers and a slightly persnickety cat. Join her newsletter to receive updates and giveaways, or be part of her Facebook groups, to discuss all manner of books. Links can be found on her website: https://katehewittbooks.com/

Her latest releases are *The Girl Who Never Gave Up* a WW2 novel based on the true story of the doomed refugee ship the St Louis, *The Midnight Hour*, the second in her dystopian series Lost Lake, and *Playing for Keeps in Starr's Fall*, the second standalone in her new heartwarming series inspired by the Gilmore Girls. There's something for everyone so do check them all out, and be in touch as Kate loves to hear from readers. You can discuss Kate's books as well as others on her private Facebook group, Kate's Reads or read her thoughts on Substack.

Printed in Great Britain
by Amazon

61337018R00107